It Only Happens in Christmas   Town

Magic Moments: Novella #2

Shirley Hailstock

Acknowledgements

To Melinda Curtis who invited me into this project. Thank you for the opportunity.

Praise and Awards

Library Journal Bestselling Author

#1 Kindle Bestselling Author

"[**Summer on Kendall Farm**]...*featuring memorable characters that are easy to like.*"

~RT Book review

"***Summer on Kendall Farm****...This is the perfect book to share...with fans of sweet, clean romances.*"

~Romance in Color

"*For anyone who's ever dreamed of doing something before it's too late,* [**Promises to Keep**] *is a book about two people who actually manage it. They let go, take off and decide to see what the road will bring them.*"

~Dear Author

Prologue

The coffee shop was virtually empty. It was the way Whitney liked it. She didn't have to speak to people or acknowledge their presence. She could drink her coffee and think or not think.

A magazine lay on the table next to her cup, a glossy star-studded periodical. She hadn't read it, hadn't even looked at the cover. . Whitney didn't read those things and couldn't remember buying this one.

She'd been forgetful lately. Distracted. Blocked. Her business…

Suddenly, something heavy plopped in front of her. Pushing the magazine aside, she looked up. A woman had dropped down on the opposite side of her table. Whitney looked around, wondering if a sudden surge of patrons had converged on the place.

They hadn't.

All but two of the tables were still empty.

The woman in front of her said nothing, but gave Whitney a short, fast smile.

"Do I know you?" Whitney asked, her voice too low for the other customers to hear her.

"I know you," the woman said. "And I know what you need."

"Who are you?" Whitney frowned. She'd never seen this woman before.

The woman had blonde hair and carried a large purse, more like a satchel. Her dress was a dark, indistinct color. Once it had been black or possibly green. Now it was a muted grey. Her hair wasn't totally in place, and it lay limp. Bohemian bracelets bangled at her wrists.

"My name is Edith Potter, and I'm here for you."

"For me? Are you a cop or something?" Whitney had done nothing to warrant a cop's attention, but why else would the woman say she was here for her?

Edith laughed. "Do I look like a cop?"

She didn't, but Whitney hadn't understood what *being here for her* meant.

"I have two things for you, and they must be done before Christmas."

"Christmas? This is June." Whitney leaned closer, despite her apprehension that she was sitting across from a mental patient.

"So you've got six months." Edith handed her a long red and white striped stocking. "Look inside."

"What's this?" Whitney asked.

"It's what you need to make things right again." With that, the woman got up and left. Whitney stared after her for a moment. Who was this woman and how could a sock fix all that had gone wrong in the last year.

Whitney wanted her life to get back on track. Inside the stocking was a folded piece of Christmas notepaper. It held a few numbers and letters. It was some kind of code, but to Whitney it meant nothing.

Looking up, she opened her mouth to call to the woman, but she was gone. Whitney hadn't heard the bell on the door ring. It wasn't even vibrating from a recent exit. The only people in the restaurant were her and the two other strangers.

Catching the attention of the cook behind the counter, she asked, "Do you know who that was?"

He looked around. "Who who was?"

"The woman with the large purse and grey dress."

His mouth turned down in a grimace and his shoulders hunched and dropped. "Didn't see her."

Whitney looked down at the paper in her hand. For a moment she felt as if she'd dreamed the woman up, but the paper was proof she'd been there.

"Why do I need this?" she murmured, but there was no one to answer her. Finishing her coffee, she left the slip of paper on the table and headed for the door.

This time the bell tinkled as Whitney opened and closed it.

Chapter 1

Longitude and Latitude, who uses terms like that outside of the military?

Whitney Emerson had never been in the Navy. Living in Redmond, New York, two hundred miles east of Lake Erie and even farther than that from the Atlantic Ocean, she wasn't close to a large body of water. But she was on the road to someplace in Maine that apparently had no name on the map. The GPS found the location, but as Whitney had learned, Global Positioning Satellites weren't foolproof. Thank heaven she was almost there. Snow had begun early in the day and made deeper and deeper drifts the farther across the state she drove.

Whitney had tried to explain it to herself, but there was no explanation. Somehow the paper she'd left on the table in the coffee shop in June had followed her home. It was crazy. She knew that, but when she got back to her apartment, she'd tripped on the rug and dropped her purse. As she retrieved the contents, the slip of paper lay open next to a tube of lipstick and a ballpoint pen.

For the next six months, try as she might, life had been an uphill battle. The greeting card business she'd started was flagging. She couldn't seem to find bright, cheerful words people wanted in a card. She'd been engaged to Mike for years. She'd been a party of two for three years. And now she was alone. Missing Mike. Wondering what would have happened if she'd been faster or stronger. Blaming herself for what happened.

And the slip of paper? Once she'd seen the code, she couldn't get it out of her mind. That woman's warning that she needed to do two things by Christmas nagged at her to the point that she would lose her mind if she didn't figure out what that code meant.

Finally, she plugged the numbers into a search engine and a map came up. Still, there was no place name. She was only looking at a longitude and latitude location. They had to mean something.

And Whitney was going to find out.

Two things the woman had said. This had to be one of them. At least she hoped it would lead to something better than the last year had given her.

Snow pelted the windshield like icy fingers tapping against the glass a week before Christmas. She'd driven far today. Checking the road sign coming up, she slowed enough to read it. She could have stopped dead in the middle of the highway, since she hadn't seen another car for the last fifteen miles.

Her gas gauge showed practically full, so as long as she could keep the car moving, she was in no danger. But the weather was becoming treacherous. Whitney gasped when she saw the sign. *Christmas Town 4 mi.* The letters jumped out in white reflective paint from a huge green sign. Checking the GPS, Whitney confirmed that in four miles she would reach her destination.

"Christmas Town," Whitney said aloud. Was that where that gypsy fortune teller was sending her? Whitney thought of her as a fortune teller, even though she'd had no crystal ball. It appeared she could tell the future.

What a trick. The woman must have known this was the last place Whitney wanted to be. Christmas held no appeal for her anymore. Since Mike's death, Christmas only reminded her of tragedy.

By the time she turned off the highway, the snow had changed to huge fluffy flakes. It was strange, Whitney thought. She wouldn't turn back, but crossing into Christmas Town was like finding the entrance to a magical land.

Whitney mentally shook herself. This wasn't magic. She understood that. All the magic in her life had disappeared a year ago when she lost Mike.

Shaking herself, she brought her attention back to the present. The car rolled slowly through an area of shops and stores. Lighted windows glowed yellow and welcoming. She didn't see a hotel or even a motel, yet there had to be someplace for travelers to stay. Whitney couldn't spend the night in her car. She'd freeze.

No one walked the streets, and no cars other than hers marred the freshly fallen snow. *Of course not*, she thought. Sensible people were home, safely enjoying dinner or playing board games. They were living, happy, and unaware that their lives could change in the blink of an eye. Whitney knew this from personal experience.

This time twelve months ago, she'd been sitting on top of the world. What a difference a year made. Her business had been going well. She'd picked up new clients and her love life had just moved to the next level. Then the crash came, quick, unexpected, and hard to deal with. She'd discovered the cliché was true. Her ride to the top was short-lived. And her fall was long and hard. She'd lost the most important thing in the world—Mike, the man she loved, the man who'd put an engagement ring on her finger only a couple of days earlier.

Everything happened so fast. It was impossible to stop it, just as it was impossible to break away from the nightmares or from reliving the accident when she was incapable of changing the outcome. Mike was gone forever.

But this year, she was taking the gypsy's advice and changing her surroundings, seeing where gypsy Edith Potter's directions would lead. This Christmas, Whitney wouldn't remain anywhere near her home, but would go where the car took her, to a place that she and Mike had never been together. Apparently, that was Christmas Town, Maine.

~*~

Whitney looked from one side of the street to the other. She saw a small café. Pulling the car in front of it, she noticed the word *Closed* in huge block letters on the door. On a night like this, what should she expect? This was Christmas Town, obviously not a 24/7 city. She was just about to back out of the parking space when she noticed a small sign in the window. Expecting it to say *Help Wanted*, her heart fluttered when she read *Rooms to Let*.

Whitney had never seen a sign like that outside of a black and white movie. But whether it was contemporary language or not, she was going to Reindeer Avenue and see if the rooms to let were still available.

When she arrived, there was no answer to her knock or the ringing of the doorbell. Whitney looked about. The town seemed large enough that she should have found it on her map. She discarded the thought. The map was unimportant. Food and a place to sleep were what she needed.

"Is there something I can help you with?" Someone shouted from the street.

Startled, Whitney jumped as she turned. A man was coming toward her.

"I'm here to rent the room. Are you the owner?" She wanted to get out of the cold, but she wasn't sure she wanted to rent a room from this man. He looked like a polar bear in the snow, white down coat with a hood covering his head.

"The owners are at the festival."

"Festival?"

"It's the first of the season; eleven of them are held every year about this time. Everyone is there."

"When will they be back?" Whitney asked.

By now he was close enough for her to see his features. Despite the bulky white coat, he had sunburnt skin and the clearest blue eyes she'd ever seen. She was used to looking up at men, but not as far as she had to look to see his face. She stood five feet five inches in her stocking feet. She was wearing boots, but they were flat. He had to be well over six feet. Mike stood five feet eleven, although if asked he often rounded up to get the missing inch.

"Not for a couple of hours. The festival just got started."

She wondered why he wasn't there. "I saw the café in town was closed. While I wait, is there any place I could get something to eat?"

On cue, her stomach growled. Whitney's last meal had been lunch and it was after eight o'clock now.

"Yeah," he said. "I know a place."

Whitney wasn't sure. The way he said it sent chills down her spine. It was dark, she was a stranger in town, hungry, and she didn't know this man.

"The food is good," he went on.

"Is it far?" She'd been on the road since early morning and she wasn't looking forward to driving in the snow any more tonight.

"Nothing's very far in Christmas Town, but tonight is not a night for walking. I can drive you."

Whitney eyed him cautiously. "I don't think so," she said, shaking her head. Her voice was low compared to the wind blowing around them. She wasn't about to get in the truck with a man she'd only met five minutes ago. She didn't even know his name.

"Trenton Knowles," he said, almost as if he knew what she was thinking. "My friends call me Trent." He offered his hand. Whitney looked at it for a moment before putting hers in it. "Whitney Emerson." His hand tightened a little too hard and Whitney's eyes opened wider. She pulled free of his grasp.

"Well, Whitney Emerson, would you like to ride with me or follow me? I promise to be a perfect gentleman and get you back here when Margaret and Justine, the owners of the cottage, have returned."

Again, Whitney weighed her decision. She was bone tired. If she had a bed to sleep in, she'd forego eating until morning.

"Well?" he prompted.

Whitney looked around. Her car was nearly covered with snow. Behind it sat a pickup truck. She knew it was his.

"Where are we going?"

"A couple of miles from here. I'll warn you, no one else is there. We'll be alone. Do you like lasagna?"

Whitney could already taste the tomato based pasta. She nodded.

"Come on."

It was his smile that got her. She was about to take the chance that a serial killer wouldn't be lurking in a place called Christmas Town.

The truck cab was warm, and she welcomed the heat after being outside for only a moment. Trent pushed his hood back. His hair was dark and an inch longer than his collar. She assumed he didn't work in an office. The long hair, coupled with the outdoorsy look of him, told her Trent was different from the type of men she'd met in the past. Once she'd worked in an architect's office. Now with her constant flow of clients, her office was filled with neat, business-suit types.

"So Trent, why aren't you at this festival where everyone else is?"

"I was on my way when I saw a woman knocking on the door of someone I knew wasn't home."

"Oh," Whitney said. "I'm sorry to put you out."

"No problem. The festivities go on every night until Christmas, and no one is going to miss me. I'm not supposed to be here anyway."

"Really?" She looked at him skeptically. The man was handsome, especially in the soft light of the cab. Whitney would have thought he'd have women falling all over him.

"I was out of town. I'm back a day early."

He turned onto a road that led toward bright, colorful lights. Whitney gripped the door handle and gasped. The music she heard was unmistakable. It took her back years and had her heart racing."How much further is it?"

"We're here," he said.

"Here?" she echoed.

Shutting the engine off, he climbed down from the cab and came around to help her out. Whitney sat stiffly in her seat. "This is an amusement park." It was empty, but lights twinkled from the ground to the sky. "Welcome to Knowles Wonderland." He smiled proudly.

"Why are we here?" Whitney didn't move from her seat.

"This is where you'll get something to eat."

Whitney wanted to turn and run, but without a car, she was at the mercy of this man, this stranger.

"Coming?" Trent asked.

He offered her a hand and helped her to the ground. She didn't say a word. Her eyes were on the giant Ferris wheel that loomed to the sky. Like a zombie, Whitney allowed herself to be led to a trailer. The lights were on, even though he'd said they'd be alone.

Unlocking the door, he shuffled her inside. It was warm and comfortable, clean with a pleasant scent. He went straight to the kitchen area.

"Take off your coat. Make yourself comfortable."

Opening the freezer, he took out a covered dish. Removing the top, Trent put it in the microwave and pressed the *On* button. The oven began to hum as the light came on and the glass plate circled to evenly cook the food. Shrugging out of his coat, he slung it on the back of an empty chair. Whitney did the same with hers.

Without asking, he made coffee and set a mug in front of her. Adding sugar packets and creamers in mini plastic cups, obviously from a diner, made her smile.

"And here I was thinking how self-sufficient you were," Whitney commented

"You've changed your mind?"

His smile was devastating. Whitney realized she hadn't thought that about a man since Mike died. Dropping her eyes, she picked up one of the creamers.

"They always give you too many when you get coffee out," he said. "Why waste them?"

"So you're a conservationist?"

"No, just an amusement park owner."

She looked up as if she could see the park outside covered in white. "You own this park?"

"It was an inheritance, but the bank and I own it," he said.

The bell on the microwave cut off any further explanation. Trent pulled plates from a cabinet. The tomato smell of the lasagna filled the small area. She hadn't seen him put bread in the oven, but he pulled out a full loaf already buttered.

Whitney ate heartily in comfortable silence.

"More?" he offered when she'd finished the first helping.

She pushed her plate away and sat back in the chair, shaking her head. "That was delicious. Thank you. I don't often meet men who can cook."

"How do you know I cooked that?"

She took the dishes to the sink and began cleaning them. Trent turned in his chair and faced her.

"You were fast and efficient. The lasagna was homemade. I've eaten enough packaged goods to be able to tell the difference. And what guy makes garlic bread? You set the table, made coffee and had everything on the table while it was still hot. Yep, you can cook."

"When you get tired of eating out, you learn a few things, and Betty Crocker helps."

"Betty Crocker?" Whitney questioned.

Trent pulled a copy of a well-used cookbook from the top of the refrigerator. "It's the only one I own."

Trent was different from Mike. Mike hadn't been a good cook other than his skills at the barbecue. Mike had been a private person. He never would have insisted a woman come share his leftovers. Mike had lived in a high-rise apartment. Trent was confident in his cooking skills, basic as they might be. He lived in a trailer, owned an amusement park of all things, and called Christmas Town home. Mike would have been…Well, this hadn't been Mike's path.

But it was Trent's and he intrigued her. It had been a long time since she felt anything for a man. Yet, her eyes followed him. She noticed the way he looked, how he moved, the way he walked and talked, even noticed the small dimple in his left cheek and the tiny scar under his chin that might be the remnant of a childhood fall. Because his face was wind burned, the scar stood out as a short, white line.

"You have New York plates on your car. That's a long way from here. Are you heading there for the holidays?"

She shook her head. "I'm going away from New York." Away from memories, pain, and guilt.

"Spending the holidays with family?"

Whitney became uncomfortable. Ignoring his question, she asked, "Do you think the cottage owners are back yet? I'm tired from the long drive."

"Sorry. Let me give them a call." Pulling his cell phone out, he punched in some numbers, spoke for less than a minute and ended the call. "We can go," he said.

Whitney finished the dishes, dried her hands and reached for her coat. She stumbled her first step out of the door. Again, the park rides loomed in front of her like neon giants. The drive seemed shorter on the way back than it had coming in.

Margaret and Justine, two young women who were lovely enough to be fashion models, opened the door as she and Trent approached it. Both women hugged him.

After introducing Whitney and explaining about finding her, he said, "She's looking to stay for a night or two. At least until the snow stops and the roads are passable."

"We have a small cabin in the back with everything you'll need," Margaret said.

"Trent, why don't you go and get her things and take them to the cabin?" Justine looked at Whitney. "We turned the heat up after Trent's call. It might be a little cool, but it'll be warm in no time."

"I just want to get some rest," Whitney said, hoping she didn't look as tired as she felt.

"We'll get you checked in and then the place is yours," Justine responded.

Whitney registered and Trent agreed to show her the cabin. He led her to a small unit that sat behind the main house on a double lot. Whitney could only think of it as storybook cottage. It wasn't the log cabin she'd pictured, but something that reminded her of Santa's workshop. There was a small pathway that angled in an S curve to the front door. She could imagine that path bordered by colorful flowers in the summer.

The cabin had two rooms, a general one and a bedroom. The kitchen was positioned along one wall. Trent carried her bags, dropping her single suitcase near the door and setting the case holding her laptop on a desk.

"Enjoy," he said as he headed for the door.

"Trent," she said, stopping him. "Thank you...for being my knight in shining armor."

The slow smile that curved his lips melted her heart.

"Hope to see you again," he said and closed the door.

Whitney hoped she'd see him too, but she didn't think that would happen. She planned to leave in the morning. She had no other destination in mind. She was sensible enough to know she couldn't run from herself. No matter how far or how fast she tried, she'd still have all her memories, good and bad, sitting right where she'd left them--at the base of a Ferris wheel.

Then she remembered the fortune teller and that the coordinates had led her here. Why, she had yet to discover. Two things she needed to do before Christmas, the woman had said. Well she was here in Christmas Town. This was one. What was number two?

~*~

Trent slipped under the steering wheel of his truck and turned the engine on. He didn't move to change the gear. Smiling to himself, he wondered who Whitney Emerson was and what had brought her to Christmas Town? This was a place where most of the residents were born and bred. The town saw hundreds of tourists at this time of the year. She could be just another one.

But he didn't think so.

She'd bantered with him, yet there was something behind those sad eyes of hers and he wondered what it was and who had put it there.

Putting the truck in gear, he pulled away from the curb and drove over the night's newly fallen snow. He liked Whitney, and it had been a while since he had taken to any woman. Whitney intrigued him. He wanted to know more about her. He was comfortable talking to her, and if she hadn't been so tired and sleepy, he'd have sat at the table in his trailer talking to her for as long as he could.

~*~

Morning arrived, bright and sunny. Whitney pulled the

curtains back. Blinding sunlight bounced off the white snow. Squinting, she looked at the unblemished yard. Her heart lightened as a childhood memory of making angels in the snow snuck out of her subconscious. She could see herself and her mom sharing that moment. Regardless of size or age, the two of them would roll in the wet powder and laugh.

Laughter—she remembered her mother laughing. She could hear it in her head. Closing her eyes, Whitney pulled the memory closer. For a short time she held it, allowing the glow to warm her heart.

Opening her eyes, she was about to drop the curtain when something caught her eye. It couldn't be, she told herself, banging her head on the glass as she tried to get closer to the image. It was an angel, a snow angel, just like the one she'd been remembering. It couldn't be.

But it was.

Quickly dressing, she pushed her feet into her boots and opened the door. Her walkway had already been shoveled. Whitney was a light sleeper, but she hadn't heard the rhythmic scrape of metal against concrete. Feeling like Alice in Wonderland, she followed the path to the back of the cottage. The snow angel was gone. Before her the white expanse was unmarred.

"How?" she whispered to herself. Blinking and shaking her head as if to clear it, she wondered if she'd seen anything at all. Taking a long moment to survey the yard, she checked for even the minutest shadow of the angel. She saw nothing.

Retracing her path, she returned to the front of the building. Her car sat at the curb, but instead of driving into town, she decided to walk. Smiling, she knew this must be Wonderland, since walking was something she only did on a treadmill. Treading through snow, when she had the option to drive—that was new for her.

Christmas Town is beautiful, she thought. Dressed in a blanket of new fallen snow, with decorations abounding from every house. She smiled at the beauty of the place. Reaching the second block she headed for the café that had been closed when she arrived last night, and stopped dead in her tracks. There wasn't a single space that wasn't being used for something Christmassy. Strings of lights crossed the road, swinging from lamppost to lamppost. Every building was outlined and decorated in white lights or multicolored bulbs. Some twinkled; some ran in constant succession, trying to catch the one in front of it. The shops were multicolored, yet all sported some form of red, gold, green and white. They looked like Christmas presents under the huge tree that dominated the center of the square. The snow added to the postcard-like picture.

Whitney's hand went to her heart. She should have expected something like this. After all, this *was* Christmas Town. But if that second something her gypsy had foretold didn't jump out at her this morning, she was leaving. She was feeling more cheerful than she had all year, and she had a business to run.

A horn sounded behind her, causing her to jump. The truck stopped next to her, and the window on the passenger side slid down.

"You're not lost, are you?" Trent shouted, his smile flashing in the bright morning light.

She shook her head. "I was in pursuit of coffee. The cottage has a kitchen and a coffee maker, but no supplies."

"Jump in, and we'll get some together."

Whitney shook her head. "I can get it. You're obviously on your way somewhere. I assume that café is open by now."

"It's no trouble." He reached over and pushed the door open.

Refusing would be rude, and Whitney wanted to go with him. Having someone to talk to was better than being alone. She'd been alone this last year. Not that her friends hadn't rallied around her, but she'd been a party of one at restaurants. Meeting Trent last night and talking to him had made her comfortable. Maybe because he knew nothing about her or her past, he was exactly the person she needed.

"Are you all settled in?" he asked a moment after she buckled her seat belt.

"Not totally. I was considering leaving this morning."

"What? Why?"

It was flattering that he seemed to care that she stayed longer. "Christmas Town isn't my kind of place."

"What does that mean?" he asked. "Everyone loves Christmas."

Whitney shifted in the seat and looked directly at him. He was still handsome, but she had to be practical. She lived in New York. He lived here. "Look, we don't know each other well. So just let me say, it's not my favorite holiday and this..." She spread her hands to include the entire street and town. "This is obviously a place that celebrates Christmas twenty-four hours a day, every day of the year."

"It's on the tip of my tongue to ask what happened to you at Christmas. Who did you lose? Who did you break up with? But I'm not going to ask. As least not now."

The tightness in her throat at his questions eased when he backed off.

He parked in front of the Silver Bells Café and they went inside. The place was ready for Christmas. Tablecloths bore winter scenes of sledding children, red and green candles in the center, green and silver garland strung on every surface, and the tree centered in the room, forced people to walk around it.

Trent led her to a booth near the windows. She felt the warmth of his hands as he helped her with her coat. Hanging it on a hook, he stood so close she could take in the smell of him. Again she had a strange feeling. There were things that couldn't be smelled, but she felt like she caught their scent when Trent was near. Winter snow, the wind, and sunshine came to mind.

She slid into the seat. A waitress dressed as an elf came over, set two cups on the table and left a pot of coffee. She smiled at Trent, but said nothing. Whitney could tell they were friends, and he was obviously a regular here.

"Did you call an order in I don't know about?" she asked.

He shook his head. "That's Grace Bell. She owns the place. Came here one Christmas and never left."

A slow smile curved his mouth. Whitney found herself looking at the way his mouth wasn't perfectly symmetrical. The left side wasn't as high as the right. Maybe that's what gave him the dimple. Taking the pot, she filled her cup and then his.

"So, can I convince you to give the town a try before you head out?"

"Why?" Whitney was not the kind to stop and stay.

Trent seemed a little undone by her question. "For one thing, it's a great place to live. It's holiday time and everyone needs a holiday. They lift your spirit, make you want to renew life."

"You're a different kind of man," she said.

"What's different about me?"

"From my experience, women carry the holidays. They decorate. They shop, buy cards, cook the food, and bring everyone together. So far you haven't mentioned a woman, girlfriend, sister or mother. Since you're so into Christmas, there must be someone you rely on or someone you share all the joys of the season with."

"I have parents. They live in Arizona. I have a sister and a brother. One lives in Portland, the other in Vermont. An aunt lives here over in Bar Harbor."

"And a girlfriend? I don't see a wedding band, so I assume you're not married."

"Not married, no girlfriend," he said. Yet his tone told her he'd recently had one.

Whitney wanted to ask what happened, but since she was unwilling to share her past, she couldn't ask him about his.

The waitress returned and set two hefty plates in front of them.

"Is this the way it works here?" Whitney asked. She looked down at her plate. After so much pasta last night and immediately going to bed, Whitney shouldn't be hungry, but she'd been thinking of a breakfast of hot cakes, bacon, eggs scrambled with cheese, and without ordering, here it was.

"She's an elf. They can read minds, you know."

In front of Trent, she'd left French toast, sausage and eggs, and a tray of flavored syrups.

Whitney laughed. "I've never heard that."

"It only happens here in Christmas Town."

Whitney didn't know what to make of that. He was kidding,

she told herself, but the waitress had done nothing but smile, and she'd given Whitney exactly what she'd had in mind. Back in Redmond, she would rarely order such a carb-intense meal, but here it seemed right and she was hungry.

Spreading the lump of butter over the hot cakes, she added maple syrup and dug in. The food was heavenly. Her eyes closed as she savored it. Nothing she'd eaten had ever tasted better. Whitney stopped and stared at her plate. Last night's dinner of lasagna with Trent had also tasted better than any lasagna she'd ever eaten. And she'd had both meals with him.

"What do you do when you're not here?" Trent's question interrupted her musings.

"I work in a factory." She smiled.

"Doing what?"

"It's not really a factory. Not the way you think when you hear that word. I create greeting cards."

"What do you mean create? Do you write the inscriptions?"

"Sometimes." Not at all this year. "When I was in college, we had an assignment to write a jingle for a commercial."

"You were a Fine Arts major?"

She shook her head. "Mathematics. The course was an elective. It looked like fun and I enrolled. I wrote a jingle for soap powder." She smiled, remembering the silly words. "I produced it on my computer, using free music and live action videos."

"And that's how you got into the greeting card business?"

"By a circuitous route. For fun, I also wrote a Valentine's Day card. I did the same thing, setting it to music and using some images of myself during a gymnastics practice."

"Wait, you were a gymnast?"

She nodded, thinking that it was gymnastics that saved her life. Pushing the thought aside, she refused to think about that.

"The day I was to turn in the jingle," she continued. "I mistakenly sent in the card file and not the jingle."

"What happened?" He'd stopped eating.

"I can't really say how everything worked in the background. I think the professor showed it around to others and they laughed over what I'd sent in place of the assignment. Somehow the file ended up at a card manufacturer, and they offered me a job."

"Writing jingles or tumbling?" he laughed.

Whitney made a face at him.   "Writing."

"That was lucky," Trent said.

"It was extremely lucky." She took a drink of her coffee, remembering when she'd thought architecture was going to be her future. "I took the job and learned all I could. Then I decided to try it on my own."

"So you started a card company while you were still in college?"

She nodded. "Now it supports me."

Whitney looked at her plate. It was completely empty. She'd eaten everything and drank two cups of coffee. And she felt great. She should be sluggish and sleepy after putting away all that food, but she felt as if she could tackle anything.

"That's what you'll be returning to when you leave here?"

"I haven't worked the day-to-day operation since earlier this year. I have a manager who handles everything." Whitney didn't explain what happened to take her away from a business she'd been hands-on with for a decade. After Mike, she couldn't do it. Thankfully, there was her assistant, Tracy. The woman was extremely talented and efficient. She was a detail person who had a unique ability to also be creative. She'd stepped in when Whitney was away and now she managed the entire operation.

"Something happened a year ago?"

Whitney stared at him. Could everyone in this town read minds or something? It could be that they were just perceptive, that her body language gave her away, but she had the uncanny feeling that people in Christmas Town were a community unto themselves.

Chapter 2

When they exited the café, Trent opened the door of his truck, but Whitney didn't get in.

"I think I'll continue walking," she said. "I haven't seen anything of the town during daylight."

"I can give you a tour," he volunteered.

"I'd like to walk. It's picturesque, much like a postcard."

Her smile was bright, but Trent sensed her apprehension. She was holding something back. He closed the door and stepped aside. He had to return to the amusement park.

Whitney walked away. Trent watched her go, saw her stop and look in windows. She was tall and slender, but not too slender, definitely not model thin. He didn't want model thin. He wanted a woman who was real and Whitney Emerson just might fit the bill.

"Checking out the new lady in town?"

Trent swung around to see his cousin Patrick Nolan, who owned a Christmas tree farm just outside of town. "Got your eye on someone?"

"I had breakfast with her." He glanced at Whitney. She was nearly out of sight.

"And you say I fall in love too quickly." Patrick patted Trent on the back.

"This is fate." Trent rolled his shoulder.

"What makes you say that?"

"I'm not sure. All I can tell you is that a strange woman came to me last summer and gave me a Christmas stocking with a piece of paper inside. On it was written, *Emerson needs your help.*"

"And this is Whitney Emerson." Patrick looked ahead of them. Whitney was gone.

"Who was this woman?"

"I have no idea. I'd never seen her before or since. I got distracted by something in the park and when I tried to find her after I looked at what she'd written, she was gone. It was like she disappeared." Trent didn't tell him the whole truth. He left out that the woman had been sitting in a fortune teller's booth in his park. It, too, had vanished as if it never existed.

"Emerson is a common enough name," Patrick said. "It doesn't mean she's the subject of the note."

"It does," Trent said positively.

"How do you know?"

"Because there were also coordinates on the note."

"Coordinates?" Patrick questioned.

"Longitude and latitude coordinates." He stopped and looked directly at him, knowing what the next question would be. "They pointed to Margaret and Justine's doorstep and that is where I found Ms. Whitney Emerson last night."

~*~

If there was ever a show stopper, Whitney thought, *this is it*. Staring in the window of a dress shop at the end of the block, she couldn't take her eyes off the red concoction displayed there. Christmas was only a little over a week away. The streets were crowded with shoppers and tourists. They moved about her, but she was oblivious of them.

The female mannequin wore a red satin gown that nipped in at the waist and curved along all the right places. Netting arced around her shoulders creating a haze of color. Whitney wanted it. She hadn't craved a new dress or even a blouse for the past year. Existing mainly in jeans and t-shirts or sweatpants and shirts, she had refused all invitations where she could wear such a beautiful dress.

After spending a full five minutes looking at it, she decided against it and turned to leave. She didn't look first and ran directly into someone. The bump was so hard and so unexpected that she fell backwards and landed on her tailbone.

"I am so sorry," the woman said, reaching down to help her up.

Whitney got up brushing her pants off. Her butt hurt. "It was my fault," she said. "I should have been looking where I was going."

"You were looking at the gown?'

Whitney turned back to the store window. "Isn't it beautiful?"

"And it's just your size."

Whitney frowned. She looked at the woman. She was no taller than Whitney. Her complexion was perfect, smooth, even and flawless. She wore a black coat that covered all of her except the toes of the black boots on her feet. "How would you know that?"

"I'm psychic," she said with a smile that meant the opposite. "Why don't you go in and try it on?"

"I have no place to wear anything like that."

"What about the festivals? It's Christmas, and there are functions every night that call for fancy dress clothes."

"I'm not from Christmas Town. I probably won't attend any of the festivals."

"Not attend? That's out of the question. You're here. You'll love how we celebrate the season."

That was just it, Whitney thought. She didn't want to celebrate the season. "I'm afraid I'm very busy and I don't really know anyone here."

The woman took a step back and extended her hand. "Let me be the first. I'm Casey Alexander. I own the shop."

"Oh, that must be how you could estimate my size."

"Come on in. I promise if you don't want it, I won't push."

Casey didn't have to push. Once Whitney saw herself in the gown, she was in love with the dress. It was beautiful and it made her feel beautiful. More than that, she felt like Cinderella. Another fairy tale, she thought. When she left the cabin this morning she was Alice in Wonderland, and now she was Cinderella. Turning completely around, she looked at herself in the three mirrors. Every angle was perfect. The dress fit as if she'd stood in a tailor's shop and had them make it for her specific size and form.

"No one else will look as good in that dress," Casey said.

Whitney couldn't argue that. She left the shop, carrying a grey box with Casey's logo on the side. But even wearing boots and walking through fresh snow, her step was light and happy enough to go into Dockery's, a store several doors down. She bought three pairs of elf socks. She'd made up her mind. She wasn't hurrying back to her life. She was in Christmas Town for the duration, whatever that might turn out to be, and she might need socks more than she needed a new dress.

Shopping wasn't on Whitney's agenda. The sight of the dress *had* stopped her. The gown now lay on the bed of her rented cottage next to the socks. *Incongruous*, she thought, picking up a pair and laughing. Whatever had possessed her? She'd wanted a pair of elf socks for years, but never found a place that sold them when she was thinking about them. She was too tall to be an elf, but the alternating red and white circular stripes that would go around her legs were whimsical and seemed right for a place like this town. Of course, they wouldn't go with the gown, despite their colors matching perfectly.

Whitney caught a glimpse of herself in the mirror. She froze a moment, not recognizing herself. She wore a wide smile and realized how good it felt to laugh. Reaching for the gown, she wished she had somewhere to wear it.

Suddenly the phone rang, causing her to jump. It wasn't her cell, but the white touch tone phone on the night stand. It wasn't a ringtone, but a ringing that was both foreign and jarring to her ear. She hadn't heard a real ring in years or even seen a touch-tone phone this old. Whitney stared at it through two rings. No one knew she was here. Anyone looking for her would call her cell.

Lifting the receiver, she raised it to her ear with all the deliberation she would if it were about to explode.

"Hello," she said tentatively.

"Whitney?"

"Yes," she said, not recognizing the voice. "Who is this?"

"Trent," he said.

Trent, of course, she thought. Who else could it be?

"Are you still there?" Trent asked.

"I'm here." Whitney sat on the bed, crushing the dress, unsure why her heart suddenly began to beat faster.

"I mentioned the festival tonight."

"One of eleven," she said. "I remember."

"Since you don't know our little town, I thought you might like to go."

Whitney didn't know if she wanted to get so deeply entwined with the permanent residents. Her life was in Redmond. This was only a stop on her way to someplace else. She thought it was on her way to healing. She knew she needed to get over Mike, to put what had happened into perspective. And learn why the gypsy, a total stranger, had given her a note six months ago that led her here.

She had to get better. Her life was suffering. Her business, her friendships, all were falling aside. Or in the case of her business, not moving forward. Her best friend had told her she needed help and instead of taking the therapist trip, she'd opted for the fortune teller route. That in itself was strange behavior on Whitney's part. She did not believe in fortune tellers.

Yet she was here.

"What do they do at festivals?" she hedged.

"Eat, dance, sing Christmas carols. Tonight is the first ball. You'll get to meet some of the other people in town."

"I haven't danced in a long time." Whitney used to love to dance. That was before Mike died. She wasn't sure how it would feel to dance with someone else. An image of Trent came to mind. She could see his strong arms around her, her head on his shoulder as they swayed to music. What would Mike think of her dancing with another man?

"The dance is the major focus tonight. It's formal." Trent broke into her thoughts.

Whitney glanced at her gown. She'd just been wishing she had someplace to wear it. And here was an invitation. The feeling that she wasn't in control of her destiny settled over her like a rough blanket.

"Formal?" she questioned. "And you don't already have someone to take?" That seemed unusual to her. But before he could respond, she said, "I'd love to go."

When Whitney replaced the phone, she realized she had a date.

It had been a year since she'd wanted the company of a man who wasn't a friend. She wondered if it was the town. Back in Redmond, she'd have said it was silly to think a place had any particular quality that could affect the human mind, but since that gypsy fortune teller had sat at her table, she wasn't so sure anymore. Why had she accepted Trent's invitation? He was good looking, but there were many men she knew who looked just as good or better. She knew men who were as intelligent. But with Trent, there was something more. She couldn't define it. It was more a want …no…a need to see what was possible if she could bring herself to move on.

Tonight she would dance.

~*~

Was she Pygmalion or Cinderella? Whitney couldn't decide. Whitney wore the dress for tonight, but not all the other things that went with it. And unfortunately, she couldn't conjure up a pair of glass slippers or a coat. Cinderella went out on a warm fall night. Remember the pumpkins? Whitney would be tackling a December winter in Maine. Covering her beautiful gown with a quilted-down coat was her only option until her neighbors arrived as if they were fairy god mothers. When Trent showed up, she was wearing a pair of silver sequin shoes that glittered in the light. They fit like a glove. Around her shoulders rested a white satin evening coat with a hood. Both were lined in red velvet.

"You look wonderful," Trent said breathily when he saw her.

Whitney smiled. "I had help, although I have no idea how they knew."

"They?"

"Margaret and Justine. Part of my ensemble is borrowed. And the size is perfect."

Trent nodded appreciatively. Secretly, Whitney wondered if her Cinderella fix would last, or was it destined to revert and leave her cold and shoeless at midnight?

Trent opened the door, looked at the snow on the ground and

then at her sparkling feet. "A man's gotta do what a man's gotta do." He swung her in his arms and carried her to his chariot. Whitney had never been swept off her feet before.

At the dance, she was greeted as a friend. She held onto Trent's arm as he introduced her and people came over to say hello. She lost track of everyone's name after the third set of Mr.'s and Mrs.'s were presented. Music began and Trent led her to the dance floor.

"Are people here always this friendly?" Whitney asked. She wasn't used to this kind of reception. She came from a world where people kept to themselves, where you only spoke to people who were your close friends.

"I think so, but especially at Christmas time."

Turning her into his arms, Trent began to dance. Whitney thought it was going to be strange, dancing with someone other than Mike. But Trent's arms were tight and just as sure around her. He guided her about the floor with ease as Mike had done. She was able to follow Trent's steps without effort. In fact, she thought matching what he did, backwards and in heels, was natural.

"You look happy," he said, staring down at her.

Whitney blushed, turning her face down. She rested her head on his shoulder as the two of them circled the room. She remembered putting on the dress and longing to dance. And now she was doing her best Ginger Rogers. She hadn't been happy in a long while, but she realized that she did feel better. Was this town insulating her from her past loss? If it was, she wouldn't question it. This feeling was much better than any emotion she'd had prior to crossing into the city limits.

Trent's head pressed against hers. She closed her eyes, savoring the moment and allowing the music to carry her away.

After a while, she looked up. "Have you always lived here?"

He nodded. "My family goes back generations. I spent a few years at the University of Connecticut and there's the occasional vacation, but for the most part, I call Christmas Town my home."

"And you like living here?" It was decadent to dream of living here year round and feeling her burdens had been lifted.

He smiled, but his mouth held a question. "Who wouldn't want to live in a place where it's Christmas every day?"

"There's more than that, isn't there?" Whitney asked.

His brows rose. "What do you mean?"

"How does this town work?" she asked.

"I don't understand the question. It works like any other town, I suppose. I run the amusement park and pitch in as a volunteer fireman. We have all the same services, police, fire, hospital, public works, you name it."

"Is there something different, something more invisible?"

"You mean like ghosts and things that go bump in the night?"

"Not exactly, and day or night doesn't matter. It seems that there are things happening here I don't understand."

"Like what?"

"Like I just think of things and they somehow happen."

"What are you thinking of now?" he teased.

Whitney knew he was trying to lighten the mood descending heavily around them. "I'm serious," she said. "I want to know how this town works its…its…"

Trent turned with his arm around her waist and walked her off the floor. They stopped at the edge of room, near a set of large windows and out of earshot of anyone else.

"What's happened?" he asked, his voice full of concern.

"Nothing bad," she said. "Just that I'm not used to having things happen to me that I can't explain."

"Like what?"

"Well," she hesitated. "Let's start with breakfast this morning. I didn't order anything, not even coffee, but the waitress put a plate in front of me that had exactly what I was thinking of eating. And then this dress."

"You thought of this dress?"

"No, I saw it and thought of having a place to wear it. A moment later, the phone rang and you asked me out. When I hung up, I realized I had no coat and no shoes to go with it. And at my door, Margaret and Justine appear with the exact items I need. And they fit like they were made for me." She glanced at her feet then looked at him for an explanation. "There's got to be something going on here."

"There's nothing going on."

"Then how do you explain these things?"

"You didn't have to order breakfast because it's a very popular breakfast and I order it all the time. Maybe you saw the picture in the window or on the menu and unconsciously wanted that breakfast because it's something you'd never order back where you came from."

That was logical. She couldn't remember seeing a photo, but that didn't mean it wasn't there. She had been more distracted by Trent at the time.

"What about the dress? The coat? The shoes?" She looked down at the glittering sequins covering her feet.

"You said you wanted the dress," Trent said.

"I did, but the woman on the street, the one who owned the shop, she knew before I even went into the shop that the dress would fit."

"She's owned that shop for years. She's good at judging sizes. Even with your coat on, she could probably determine a size that was close enough. As for the shoes and coat, I ran into Margaret and Casey and told them I was taking you to the festival. Casey mentioned the dress, but said you hadn't bought shoes or a coat to go with the gown, which is beautiful, I might add. Margaret agreed to take you the two items on a returnable basis. Satisfied?"

Whitney wanted to disagree, but she couldn't. The explanation was logical and she could just be seeing things that weren't there. Yet in the back of her mind, something still worried her that all was not as it should be.

Chapter 3

Whitney seemed to accept his explanation. They danced and talked for the rest of the festival, and she looked better than when she'd first come to town. What Trent told her was technically true. He didn't think there was anything going on in town, nothing unusual that is. It wasn't a place of witches or spells. The only magic within the city limits was Christmas magic.

"Tired?" he asked, helping her into her consigned coat.

"I could have danced all night," she said.

"Well, I'm not Professor Higgins, but I'm glad Christmas Town looks good in your eyes."

"It is beautiful. I walked around this morning and everything is crisp and clean. The decorations are so life-like they could be alive."

"Didn't you expect that when you decided to come to a place with this name?"

"I didn't exactly know where I was going," she said. "I entered the coordinates into my GPS and it led me here."

"Coordinates. That sounds like a military location," Trent said. "Where did they come from?"

She didn't answer. She was staring at the park as he pulled into the parking lot.

"Why are we here?" she asked.

He'd driven her to the place he loved most, wanting her to share in his enjoyment of it."I guess I just drifted. The night's calm, not too cold, full moon even." They both looked up at the sky. "It's natural for me to gravitate here." Trent started to get out. Whitney grabbed his arm. He turned back. "Something wrong?"

The place was open as it was every night until Christmas. The light shows were on. The indoor movies about Christmas were playing. Visits to Santa Claus had ended at nine, but the thousands of lights that wound around every tree and building on the thirty-acre track were on wondrous display. Tourists were inside in large groups. Laughter accompanied the swinging revolutions of some of the rides.

"Can you take me home? I'm not in the mood for a park tonight."

"Of course," Trent said, but he had the feeling there was another explanation. Something in there scared her. He didn't know what, but many people were afraid of amusement rides. He hadn't thought of taking her on a ride, only walking around a bit. The sidewalks were freshly shoveled. "What's it like where you're from?" he asked.

"Not like this."

"Big city?"

She nodded. "In the scheme of things, I guess you'd call it moderately sized. You won't know everyone, like you do here. Your neighbors tend to be private, but not unfriendly."

"Is that where your company is?"

She nodded. "It started out in my apartment. As it grew, I had to hire people so I took space in a small building. We outgrew that in a year and moved to larger surroundings."

"Who's taking care of it while you're here?"

"I have a wonderful manager. She'll be there until the twenty-third, then we close until the new year."

"I would think this was a busy time for a card company."

"Actually, this is a slow period. Christmas card orders went out in October. Valentine's Day and Mother's Day cards are ready to ship. We're working on Father's Day and Graduation now." Her voice trailed off, as if she'd realized there was a problem with the Father's Day and Graduation cards. And then she changed the subject.

"Don't you have to plan new rides, new...?"

He put a lot of thought into the park and his investments. "The only real thing I plan for well in advance is the Christmas season." He attended conventions for new amusements and new technology, so he supposed he did do the same things she did. Only his plans were less defined. He didn't want to turn the conversation into who did more for their business.

"It hasn't all been easy for me," she admitted, her tone still distant. She looked out the window and he couldn't see her face. "This last year…The things I've done so easily…It's been very hard."

She'd avoided talking about whatever had happened in her life to make her stumble. How he hoped they'd build a bond where no topic was taboo. "You know, one tourist in the park last year asked me if Christmas Town could be seen from space."

"What did you tell them?"

"Of course, I don't really know, but if that town in Australia can be seen, I'm sure a place dedicated to peace on earth and goodwill toward men can be seen from space."

Whitney smiled and squeezed his arm. Trent covered her hand with his own. He glanced over and their eyes met. Trent didn't understand his reaction to her. He wanted to pull over and hold her close. Instead, he returned his attention to the road.

"Why did you decide to come to Christmas Town?" he asked. "How did you program your GPS if you didn't plan to come here?"

She stiffened slightly. Trent saw it, although her movement would have been lost on anyone not looking for it.

"I'm not sure," she answered.

He waited for her to explain what she meant.

"I was in a restaurant when a woman came to my table and told me this was where I needed to be."

"Why?"

"I don't know. It was summer when she told me. I ignored her. I'd never seen her before nor since."

"But you came." Trent was interested. He forced his hands to relax on the steering wheel. He wondered if the woman she mentioned was the same stranger who'd appeared in a booth at the park. Like Whitney said, he hadn't seen her before or since.

"I came."

"Why?"

"Something happened a year ago. I'd rather not go into, but I needed to get away. And after all these months, I couldn't shake my curiosity. So I plugged these coordinates into my GPS and headed East."

"Destination unknown?"

She smiled. "It was an adventure. At least I looked at it that way. I never expected the place to be called Christmas Town."

"Didn't the GPS tell you?"

She shook her head. "I checked every map I could find and nothing had this town on it. And I didn't know if I needed to be in a place where they celebrate Christmas."

"Because of the thing you don't want to go into?" he questioned.

She nodded.

Trent stopped the car in front of Margaret's house. There was no separate driveway to reach the small cottage in the back. He got out and came around the hood to open Whitney's door and help her out. And by help her out, he meant he swept her into his arms as he had begun the evening, carrying her to her rental.

"I had a wonderful time tonight," Whitney said when he deposited her at her door.

"And do you think that happened because you wished it?"

She stared at him for a long moment. A slow smile curved her mouth. "I did wish it," she said. "And it came true."

"I wished it too," he said. "Do you want to know what else I wished?"

She nodded.

He reached down and took her face in his hands. Slowly, he pulled her toward him until his mouth was an inch from hers. She didn't pull back, her eyes didn't waver. He wondered if she was wishing the same thing he was as his mouth closed the small gap between them and he brushed his lips over hers.

~*~

Whitney opened the door and they went into the cottage. The way she felt, she really could have danced all night. She wanted to be in Trent's arms. His kiss was soft at first. He held her close, threading his fingers through her hair, while his mouth worked magic on her senses. She had wondered what it would be like to have him kiss her, but her thoughts hadn't focused on what she would feel, how affected she would be by the touch of him.

She wanted to see him again. He didn't know it, but he was helping her get over Mike's death. Just by being with her, he helped.

"I suppose you work all day tomorrow?" she asked. "The crowds are said to get denser each day."

"They do. I'll have to be at the park along with all the workers. Will you come by? Maybe for lunch or dinner?"

Whitney didn't want to go to the park. "You've provided me with an emergency dinner and a breakfast. Proper manners dictate that I return at least one of the invitations."

"I accept," he said.

She laughed. "How about dinner tomorrow? Seven o'clock?"

"I'll see you then." He leaned down and kissed her again. This time it was quick, but the thrill that went through her was just as thrilling.

Whitney hummed *I Could Have Danced All Night* as she closed the door. Then she waltzed across the room, dancing in her beautiful shoes and watching her coat fly out in a circle around her feet. Catching her reflection in a mirror, she stopped and looked. She hardly recognized herself. Gone were the dark circles under her eyes. Her face glowed with health. Part of it could be from the cold weather, but it wasn't that cold. Her hair was disheveled, giving her the look of a woman who'd been kissed.

She smiled widely.

Was Trent the reason she was here? Had the woman known that sending her here would help her get over the shock of losing her fiancé? Suddenly, Whitney's smile fell. A huge rock of guilt settled on her. She'd been happy for a few hours—without Mike. She'd been pledged to marry him and here she was dancing and feeling like a woman in love, while the man she thought she'd spend her life with was no longer part of her living circle.

Was it all right? People had told her she had to go on. She'd heard all the platitudes, messages of hope and clichés about doors closing and windows opening. None of it helped her get past the fact that she was alive and Mike was gone. But it wasn't Mike that she'd thought of since she came to Christmas Town. Trent had been her savior that first night and since then he'd been the man in her thoughts.

And now he'd kissed her.

Her hand went to her lips. She could still feel the pressure of his mouth on hers. And she couldn't help herself.

She liked it.

And she wanted him to kiss her again.

~*~

It happened the moment he walked through the door the following evening. Seven o'clock sharp. He kissed her. Even with flowers and a bottle of wine in his hands, he kissed her.

"I've been waiting all day to do that," he mumbled against her mouth.

Whitney had too, but she didn't say it aloud. She just folded herself into his arms and let them wrap her in a world she hadn't known existed. They stood that way for a while. Then she pushed back.

"I need to check on the food."

He released her. Without a word, he handed her the flowers and wine.

"Why don't you open the wine?" she suggested.

She took the flowers to the kitchen counter. Trent followed her. Handing him the corkscrew, she filled a vase and added the flowers. Setting them on the table set for two, she checked on the food.

"It smells good in here," Trent said. "So a corporate executive also knows how to cook."

"I wasn't always a corporate executive. Remember, I started the company from my apartment. Selling that first jingle helped me pay the rent. Eating out wasn't part of the equation. So I cooked for myself." Picking up an oven mitt, she asked. "How do you like your steak?"

"Medium," he answered.

She smiled. That was exactly how she liked hers. Bending down, she removed the Prime Rib from the oven and sliced it before adding it to two plates. She hoped he liked vegetables. She added them to both plates and carried them to the table. Trent poured the wine and they sat.

"To Christmas," he toasted.

"To Christmas," Whitney repeated, clinking her glass to his.

Whitney put her glass down and dug into her steak. Closing her eyes, she savored the taste of the meat.

"Wow, this tastes better than I've ever had it before. In fact, everything I eat here tastes better than it has before. Maybe there's something in the water," she laughed.

Trent bit into his. "It could be. This is delicious."

"Do you have to go back to the park after this?" she asked, refusing to say the word 'amusement'.

"I'm afraid so."

"You never told me how you got into that business. I mean you said you inherited it, but what made you want to manage it yourself?"

"It was fun when I was a teenager. All the girls wanted to be my friend."

"And now that you're old?"

"It's still fun most of the time. Parks take a lot of maintenance and I'm the lead engineer who has to make sure everything is working properly."

"Don't you have a manager?"

"Three of them. Sometimes that doesn't feel like enough, but we've had very few accidents, nothing serious."

That's good to know, Whitney thought. "What about women? The looks you were getting at the dance last night weren't lost on me."

"I'm friendly with them, but nothing serious is going on. What about you? Is there someone back in Redmond waiting for you to return?"

She thought of Mike. "There is no one waiting." Her voice was lower than usual.

"You say that like you're alone in the world. Do you have any siblings? And your parents; do they live close to you?"

"I'm alone," she said. "I was an only child and I lost my parents when I was a barely out of my teens."

"Have you ever been married or engaged?"

She took a long time to answer. Emotions still clogged her throat when she thought about Mike. "Never married," she said.

"Does that mean you were engaged?"

She nodded.

"I take it that didn't end well."

Whitney left it at that. She neither agreed nor refuted his comment. Their relationship had ended badly, but not in the way he thought. They didn't argue, fight and call things off. But, nevertheless, she was no longer engaged.

"What about you? Engaged or married?"

"Once," he said. "We got all the way to the rehearsal dinner before we decided it wasn't going to work." He looked up at her. "We were friends, had always been friends. It was expected that we would marry, but we realized in the knick of time that being friends was better than being married. So we did the right thing."

"Was she from here?"

He nodded. "She took the honeymoon cruise we were booked on with her brother. When they returned they moved to Minnesota and started a business with a man they met on the ship. She's married to him now and they have three children." He smiled. "All girls. We still keep in touch. Like I said, we're friends."

It was a heartwarming story. Whitney felt her face grow warm, not from embarrassment or fear, but from knowing someone was happy.

They finished the meal and Whitney went and got their dessert. "I didn't ask if you ate dessert," she said as she placed a dish of apple crisp with ice cream in front of him.

"Why wouldn't you think I liked dessert?"

"You're so–" She stopped, realizing she was about to comment on his body.

"So what?" he prompted.

"Well, you appear to work hard on keeping yourself fit. Usually people who do that, don't add sugar to their diet."

"Have you seen Candy Cane Lane?" he asked.

Whitney laughed. "For a moment I forgot where I was."

"You should do that more often."

His tone changed and she looked up at him. "Do what more often?"

"Let it go." He put his fork down and leaned forward. "There's something that holds you back. I've seen it more than once. You'll begin something, then you suddenly pull back as if you stepped on a nerve."

Whitney lost her appetite. Pushing back from the table, she stood up. She walked to the living room area, with Trent on her heels.

"What is it?" he asked, his voice low and full of concern.

"I don't want to talk about it."

Trent didn't say anything. She had her back to him, but she could feel his closeness. When his hands came down on her shoulders, she stiffened, then relaxed. They were heavy at first, but reassuring. She leaned back against him. She wanted to tell him, but she didn't know how. His arms slipped around her, cocooning her shoulders. Whitney felt both his tenderness and his strength.

Bending his head, he kissed her shoulder. Turning around, she was practically toe to toe with him. He didn't move to touch her further. Whitney knew he was waiting for her to make the next move. An awkward silence developed and she had no way out of it.

Trent pulled her close and brushed his lips against her temple. Then he stepped back.

It was her move and she knew it. She had to say something.

"So you want me to go," he said.

Slowly, she shook her head. Glancing through the window, she imagined the spinning lights of the Ferris wheel. Turning back, Trent slipped his hands down her arms and linked them with her fingers.

"It's the park," he said. It was not a question or a sentence. "What's up with the park?" Trent asked. "Every time I invite you there, or we get close to it, you find an excuse not to go, not to even look at it."

"It's nothing personal," Whitney said." I'm just not into amusement parks. Many people don't like the thrill rides or the noise and lights."

"But that's not you, is it? What happened to you in a park?" he asked. "Obviously something happened because your hands are ice cold and it's not cold in here. Your face looks like it came from Vampires Are Us."

Whitney waited a long moment. She was trying to get the words straight in her head. She needed to be able to relate the story without reliving it. If she couldn't, she'd burst into tears, and she didn't want to do that.

"I nearly died," she said.

"When? Where?"

"In an amusement park. A few Christmases ago." She stopped and swallowed. "I was on a Ferris wheel." Hiccups threatened to incapacitate her. Whitney swallowed them. "My fiancé was with me. Something happened—to the mechanism—and we got stuck. We were there for an hour before anything they did made the wheel turn. Then it jerked. The safety bar came..."

She dropped her head, looking at her hands, which were twisting her shirt as if it was sopping wet and needed squeezing out.

Trent took her hands. "Go on," he said.

"Mike fell. I grabbed for him and I fell out too. But...but I caught the swinging bar." Instinctively, her training as a gymnast sured her hands and they closed around the metal cylinder. "It swung away from the chair. I was above the park with nothing under me but air. The bar couldn't take my weight and it began to bend."

"Wasn't anyone coming up to get you down?"

"I don't know. I looked down and all I could see was Mike on the ground. I tried to get back to the seat, but the bar was no longer stable."

"You fell," Trenton filled in, his eyes large in his face.

She shook her head. "Not then. I swung out and hooked one leg around a support beam. Then I had to let go, but I was unsure. The bar was pulled wide and I was straining to keep hold of it and the support beam."

Trent's hand rubbed hers. "It's all right," he said. "Take your time."

"One of them had to go. I knew the bar wouldn't hold me and there was no place to go except the ground. I let go and tried to grab the beam, but I missed."

Trent squeezed his eyes closed for a moment.

"I cut my leg on the way down. I nearly bled to death. If it wasn't for the medics already on the ground, I would have died like Mike. That's why I won't go to an amusement park or get on a Ferris wheel."

"I see," Trent said quietly. He let her go and backed away. "Thanks for telling me."

Whitney took a long breath. She felt as if a huge weight had been lifted from her shoulders. She'd related the story and she hadn't given into tears or been unable to tell it from beginning to end. She thought about Mike. It was impossible not to think of him, not to see him lying, inertly, on the ground. Not to feel like her heart had shattered when she realized he was gone.

She hadn't told Trent, but the cut to her leg was one thing. The fact that Mike broke her fall and saved her life was another.

Chapter 4

Trent knocked authoritatively on Whitney's door well after breakfast and too soon for lunch the next day.

"Come with me," Trent said when she opened it. He didn't waste time on pleasantries. He'd spent the night thinking over what she had said. And he knew he had to do something. He had to do something, or they had no chance together.

"Where?" she asked.

"To the park. It's closed. There won't be anyone there but you and me."

Trent watched as her body turned so still it could have been stone.

"After what I told you last night? You know I can't go to the park. It's the last place I want to be."

"It's the only place you need to be. You have to come with me."

He understood her better since she'd told him about her previous experience.

"It's the horse cliché, right? I've fallen so I have to get on again?"

"Sort of. But what if the next time you faced a business opportunity you held back because you were uncertain? What if the next time you wished for something and it came true you were too afraid to reach out and grab it?"

"So now you're my shrink?" Whitney backed into the room. Trent closed the door and stood in front of it.

"I'm your friend," he told her. "And I want to help."

"I don't need that kind of help. And we're practically strangers."

"I kissed you."

Color flooded Whitney's face.

"We won't go on anything. We'll just walk around."

"We've done that. The first night I was here, you took me there and we walked."

"We left the truck and went straight into the trailer to eat. Then we came out and came here. I didn't notice it then, but you barely looked at anything. I didn't find that strange since the lights were off and the park was closed by the time we came out."

"Still, I don't need to go."

But Trent knew that if she didn't go, they didn't stand a chance. He liked her, but he wouldn't give up the park for her. "I won't force you. I'll be there with you, giving you all the support you need."

"Mike is dead. My going to a park won't bring him back."

"I never knew Mike and I'm sorry he's gone, but you're not. And this accident is affecting your life. You told me things have been hard. You're not the kind of woman who lets anything stand in the way of getting the job done."

She didn't deny it. Since she'd arrived, the circles under her eyes were gone and she smiled at him often. She spoke to the tourists and townspeople, but she still kept most at a distance. Everyone except him.

"Give me your hand," he said, extending his.

She looked at it for so long, Trent wasn't sure if she'd take it. But after a moment, she placed her hand inside his.

"I won't force you," he told her again. "We'll go slowly and we can turn back whenever you want."

Whitney nodded several times.

Outside it had begun to snow again. Whitney stepped out of the cottage as if she was walking into a new world.

Trent hoped she was.

~*~

At the entrance, Whitney grabbed Trent's hand with both of hers. They stopped at the gates, and she looked around, lifting her head and studying the metal structures that rose toward the sky. In her nightmares, the Ferris wheel was a monster that chased her in the dark, tormenting her until she woke up screaming.

Whitney realized she hadn't had one bad dream since she'd

come to Christmas Town. Maybe she *was* finally healing. Then she looked up and the looping monster descended.

Trent had set the Ferris wheel to run. He took her hand and pulled her forward. "All we'll do is walk by it, and we'll go back if it becomes too much for you."

Whitney took it one step at a time. She clung to Trent's hand and after a few moments relaxed a little bit, at least letting some of the stiffness out of her shoulders. They'd begun to hurt from holding them so tightly.

"How many lights are in the park?" she asked, her voice high.

"There are thousands of them, not including the ones that are permanently on the rides."

"You should hold a contest to have people guess how many lights you have."

"That would mean we'd have to count them."

"Yeah." She tried to laugh.

"That was a nice sound," Trent looked at her. "Your laugh. You don't often share it."

"After the accident, when I got out of the hospital and could return to work, I tried to throw myself into it. I needed to be exhausted in order to sleep. So I drove myself hard. There was no time for anything other than the company, but everything was different."

"You weren't writing," he surmised.

She shook her head. "I tried writing, but I'd end up in tears. Trying to write love poems or happy messages for graduation or weddings didn't work. Instead, I went to the floor and packed boxes, ran the printing machines, loaded glitter into the hoppers for pressing onto the cards."

"That doesn't sound healthy."

"It wasn't, but I learned having a support system is a wonderful thing, even if you don't appreciate them at the time."

"And they supported your decision to come here at this time of the year?" Trent asked.

"You could say that," she replied hesitantly.

"What else could I say?"

"You could tell me the truth about this town."

"What's the truth?"

"Stop hedging. There's something strange going on here." Whitney and Trent had walked past the roller coasters and were near a huge ship that swung back and forth like a pendulum. It was stationary now, quiet and ominous even in the bright light of the day.

"Why do you think there's something strange going on here?"

"You explained away my concerns the last time I asked. And all the explanations seemed logical. But I don't buy them. The waitress is a mind-reader. The dress shop owner could have gotten my size right for the dress, but the shoes? Not a chance. People seem to get what they want just by thinking about it. So tell me, what is going on?"

Trent started to speak, but Whitney stopped him. "Don't even think of telling me everything is normal. This is the most *unnormal* place I've ever been. At every turn there's something weird. I think of a meal and that's what's on the menu. I get invited to a ball where the exact dress I buy is perfect for it. I think of snow angels and suddenly outside my window are snow angels." She paused. "And then there is you."

"Me?"

"Don't pretend. I have the feeling that our meeting was orchestrated. That I was or am supposed to meet you. I don't know if it's ordained or designed, but it's certainly not serendipity."

"Why do you think you were supposed to meet me?"

She remembered the gypsy and decided that since she'd told the truth about everything else, no need to begin lying now.

"I was visited by a gypsy fortune teller. She gave me a slip of paper with longitude and latitude coordinates on it. Three guesses as to where they led me and the first two don't count."

~*~

Trent pulled her hand through his arm and the two turned toward the trailer where he'd taken her that first night. It wasn't cold to Whitney and it should be. They'd been walking for half an hour and she didn't feel the outside temperature. Again, contrary to her expectations.

"One thing happened recently that is unexplainable," Trent said.

"What?"

"The gypsy fortune teller you mentioned."

Whitney stared at him. "You've seen the fortune teller?"

"Once. She was here."

"You mean in the park?"

Trent nodded. "I came out one night about six months ago. It was summer and the night was warm. I discovered a booth with Fortune Teller written on it. I'd never hired a fortune teller or approved a booth for one. But there she was."

"What did she look like?"

"Late fifties, long hair hanging out from a scarf. She wore faded clothes, jewelry that rattled and bright red lipstick."

"I've seen her. She was the same woman who sent me here. That slip of paper. No matter where I left it, it seemed to always be in view."

"But we couldn't have seen her at the same time. That's physically impossible," Trent said.

"So is Santa Claus, flying with eight reindeer and covering the entire world in one night."

He chuckled. "I guess you have a point."

They reached the trailer close to the entrance where they had come in.

"The odd thing is, no one else saw her. No one saw a fortune teller's booth, and there was no record of any fortune teller being hired."

They passed the trailer and climbed into Trent's truck. He drove in silence for several minutes, not long enough for the truck's heater to begin warming the interior of the cab. Yet Whitney realized she wasn't cold.

"Where are we?" Whitney asked when he pulled the truck into a long driveway lined with luminaries. She imagined what they'd look like after dark.

"I live here," he said.

"I thought you lived in the trailer."

He shook his head. "I stay there sometimes when the park is busy, but I live here."

"Why did you take me there that night and not here?" The night she came. The night she needed help. It was minor help, not life threatening, but he'd come to her rescue nonetheless.

"I'd been there earlier and I keep food there in case I don't get the chance to go home."

The house was a huge brick colonial with a porch. Everything was outlined in lights.

"Do the Christmas lights stay up year round?"

Trent gave her that lazy smile. "If they didn't, it wouldn't be Christmas Town."

Whitney recognized the town's mantra. She was getting used to it, but slipped occasionally to ask a question where that was the obvious answer.

Jumping down from the cab, she followed him to the door and they went inside. It was warm, yet Whitney felt a sudden cold go through her only to be replaced by the warmth of the house's heating system. She supposed she was going to have to get used to the nuances of Christmas Town. All the cold she didn't feel while outside descended on her, then passed on as the warmth took its place. That was the only way she could describe it.

Whitney wondered about the inside decorations. Did they too remain in place every day of the year?

"No, Whitney," Trent said. She had the feeling he had read her mind.

"We don't keep everything up all the time. And the question was on your face. I didn't and can't read yours or anyone else's mind."

She smiled, feeling a little foolish...and a little relieved.

"It's beautiful." She turned completely around, looking up at the vaulted ceiling and the Christmas tree that was almost as tall. It *was* beautiful, Whitney realized. It has been a year or more since she'd appreciated Christmas and what it meant. But standing here, she remembered past years when she'd looked forward to Christmas with wide-eyed excitement...before her parents died, before she'd planned a wedding, before her life changed.

"You're smiling," Trent said, breaking into her thoughts.

"I was thinking about the tree." She took a step toward it, admiring how perfect it looked. Even though it was daytime, the lights twinkled. "We used to put ornaments on it that my parents kept for generations. We also had the torn papers ones that we were so proud of, but were only pieces of construction paper with grammatically poor writing on it."

They laughed.

"Since you're talking about Christmas trees, I have a project for you." Trent took her hand and led her into a smaller room.

Whitney looked around. This room wasn't like any of the others she'd seen. There wasn't a single Christmas decoration, candle, or themed ceramic in the space.

"What's this?" she asked.

"This is your room."

Whitney's eyes opened wide and her chin dropped. "My room?"

"Yours to decorate."

She grinned. "Part of my therapy?"

"You do several jobs at your company..." He spread his hands. "Besides, I'd bet you didn't decorate for Christmas at your house."

He took several steps toward the door.

"Are you leaving me?"

"I have to go back to the park." He put his hand on the doorknob.

"How do you know I'll do this? Or that I won't explore your home and steal everything in it?" She was kidding, but her point was that he didn't know her at all and he was leaving her alone—in his house.

"Trust," he said. "It's the basis for everything." Pulling the door open, he went through it.

"At least tell me where the decorations are?" She shouted to the empty room, listening for an answer. None was forthcoming.

Whitney turned around, much the same way as she had in the previous room. The unadorned pine tree stood in front of an array of three windows. There was a fireplace with bookcases on both sides of it. On the opposite side of the room, she spotted a box under a table. Pulling it out, she discovered the decorations. The tree already had lights on it, tiny white ones. What else, she thought. The entire town seemed to have found the manufacturer of tiny white lights. Or maybe the town had a business that produced them, although she hadn't seen it.

Unpacking the box, she put the ornaments on the table where she'd found the box. Whitney hadn't decorated a tree in years. She used to love doing it and found that the packages of red and green ribbons and the colorful figurines had her smiling.

Touching each ornament was like bringing back Christmas, one memory at a time.

She started with the tree, alternating the glass balls that had snow scenes inside them with ones that were blank until they covered the tree in lines of interchanging colors. Finding garland, she surrounded the tree with gold. The effect was heartwarming and Whitney went on. It seemed the box of decorations never emptied. Laying boughs of pine along the mantle caused fragrance to spread throughout the space. She dotted the mantle with candles, stockings and more lights.

Standing back, she surveyed her handiwork. A smile curved her lips. The room had taken on an added warmth and glow that had been missing before she began its transformation. But it needed something more. Before she could decide what it was, the door opened and in walked a woman who looked as if she was cut from the pages of a 1930's Saturday Evening Post. If Whitney had to choose a Mrs. Santa Claus from a show of a hundred, this woman was the hands down winner. White blonde hair full of curls, but lacking a bun, combined with twinkling eyes. A dress of red with a long white apron and the smell of cinnamon and sugar followed in her wake.

"I'm Mrs. Hamilton, and I believe it's time you had something to eat." She spoke as if she already knew who Whitney was.

"Whitney–"

"Emerson," she finished. "Trent has spoken of nothing but you for a while now."

She looked up and smiled at Whitney. "I'll set this here." She put the tray on the low table in front of the sofa and left the room with the same amount of sound the Ghost of Christmas Present would make.

Whitney was suddenly ravenous. She pulled the napkin from the plate and found a collection of sandwiches, all with the crust cut away. There was a pot of peppermint tea that had Whitney inhaling deeply when she smelled the familiar sweet scent. For dessert, as if the tea wasn't enough, there was a piece of cake that had been decorated like a huge tree ornament. Whitney thought about all the carbs on the tray and sat down to eat everything.

What is it about this town, she wondered, that had her doing and eating things she wouldn't even consider if she was back in Redmond? She hadn't gained any weight. Her clothes still fit the way they should, but she was going to have to pull back. No matter how good everything tasted, she would be returning to the real world. That gypsy might have told her this was where she needed to be, but she hadn't said this was where she needed to stay.

The thought of leaving made her a little sad. She thought of Trent and his smile when all around him was the joy of the holiday. He ran a place where he could see and hear smiles and screams of delight. Her work, while seasonal, was stressful and needed constant oversight.

Whitney brought her attention back to the room. She'd eaten and held a cup of tea as she went back to checking the room for what she felt needed to be done. Then she saw it. Going to the table, she removed all the boxes. Finding a white tree skirt, she folded it and covered the table, than added a mirror and covered the surface with a holiday scene. She added figures in ice skates to the mirror, some miniature buildings, trees, and carolers.

Finishing, she couldn't believe how much it reminded her of home; not the one of her childhood, but the place in Redmond where she lived now. If she'd decorated it before leaving, it would look like this. Whitney went to the fireplace, lit a fire and took a seat in front of it. The room was almost perfect.

She curled up in the corner of the sofa, her head resting on the arm. The fire flickered and danced, hypnotizing her until her eyes drooped. When she opened them, she was too comfortable to move. The light had changed. It was darker and the tree glowed. She smiled at the way it transformed the room. It was almost perfect, she thought for the second time.

Then the door opened inward, and Trent came in carrying a bottle of wine and two glasses.

Now it was perfect.

~*~

Trent looked about, his eyes going from one side to the other and taking in all the places in between. It was beautiful. It looked exactly as he'd imagined Whitney would decorate it. Like a Christmas card. The sun was setting, casting long streams of light through one set of windows while the lights from the tree and the fireplace bathed the other half. The effect was warm and welcoming. He inhaled the pine scent and appreciated her work.

Whitney, curled up on the sofa, added the exact touch the room needed. "I like it," he said.

Whitney uncoiled her legs and slipped her bare feet to the floor. She stood up, smiling.

"Did you enjoy doing it?" he asked.

"More than I ever thought I would."

He could see the pride on her face and hear it in her voice.

"And my silver and gold, is it still in place or shall I call the police?"

"I used it all." She kept her face straight, but Trent saw she was struggling. Finally, she laughed, her hand extending to encompass the tree. The gold garland and silver ornaments reflected the lights. "I did leave the frankincense and myrrh where it was. The containers were too heavy to sneak out the door." She winked at him.

"I appreciate that. Let's drink a toast to your honesty and your ability as a Christmas decorator." He set the glasses on the table in front of the sofa and opened the wine. Pouring two glasses, he handed one to her. "If you want a job, I can put in a good word for you."

Shaking her head, she said, "I don't think so."

Trent clinked her glass.

"It's a good thing your housekeeper brought me something to eat or this would go straight to my head."

Trent took a drink. "What housekeeper?"

"Mrs. Hamilton. She brought in the tra–" Whitney stopped in mid-sentence.

"What's wrong?"

"It's gone." She pointed at the table. The place where he'd set the bottle of wine.

"What's gone?"

"The tray. She brought sandwiches and tea. Peppermint tea. A dessert that looked like an ornament."

"Are you serious?"

Trent knew those were the wrong words the moment they came out of his mouth. Whitney's reaction confirmed it. It was impossible to unsay them.

"I mean–"

"Don't," she stopped him. "She must have come and gotten the tray when I dozed off."

"I don't know a Mrs. Hamilton."

"You can't miss her. She looked like Mrs. Santa Claus, someone you'd pull out of central casting, white blonde hair, red dress, long white apron."

Trent shook his head. "No one looking like that works here. I have a cleaning service that comes in once a week. Other than that I take care of the place myself."

"It's time I left this place," Whitney said. "I'm not supposed to be here. Not unless I'm supposed to lose my mind."

She went to the chair where her coat lay and slipped her arms into it.

"Don't do that." Trent stopped her from winding her scarf around her neck. He took it and dropped it back on the chair. Then he pushed her coat down her arms and settled it with the scarf. Taking her hand, he brought her back to the sofa and handed her the glass of wine. "We'll just sit here and enjoy the beautiful way you've transformed this room."

"Let's not," she said. "I only got to see the one room and this one. Why don't you give me a tour of the house?"

He stood up and offered her his hand. Whitney took it and stood. For a moment they stared at each other. Trent dropped his gaze to her mouth. He wanted to kiss her. He settled for pushing a lock of hair back from her face and brushing her cheek with the back of his hand.

Chapter 5

Eight bedrooms, seven baths, and a kitchen with a wall of windows containing sixty panes. On the small shelves of some of the panes were ceramic Christmas scenes. Each room had a Christmas tree or a scene. Whitney wondered why the one room she decorated had been left that way. Did someone somehow know that she needed to renew her faith in the holiday, and changing that room would help her see what she'd been doing to herself?

They stopped in the dining room. She saw it could seat twelve people if the chairs explained the missing table leaves.

"Do you live here alone?" Whitney hadn't seen any evidence that any of the rooms were occupied except Trent's.

"Most of the time," he said. "I have three siblings, a brother and two sisters who show up at odd times and use the house."

"What about your parents? Are they coming here for the holidays?"

"The entire lot of them will be here in a few days."

"Sounds like you'll have a lot of fun."

"We do. And most of the people who don't have family nearby celebrate with us. The park is closed on Christmas day so we get together here and have a huge party."

"One of those eleven festivals?"

He nodded. "It's always here."

"Is that why every room is decorated for Christmas?"

"The decorations make the place cheery. The party is downstairs. Only family will see the bedrooms."

Whitney pictured it. She hadn't had a family like that since she was just out of her teens. That was when she'd lost her parents. When everyone at college went home for the holidays, she remained on campus with the students from foreign countries who either didn't celebrate the holiday or found the trip home too expensive for such a short period of time.

They would do something—pretending to be having a good

time and not missing their families—but they all knew it wasn't how they really felt. When she met Mike, everything changed. She knew she was having those same feelings for Trent.

And it scared her.

Suppose she fell in love with him. What would happen? He owned the same kind of place that had taken her fiancé and nearly took her life. She couldn't go through that again.

It was time to go home, back to Redmond.

But going home didn't have the same feeling it had when she'd left. She wasn't the same person, and she could thank Christmas Town and Trent for the new her. When she got back, she'd pull out her decorations and put them up. She smiled, thinking of what her living room and her office at the factory would look like after she transformed them with bright red and green colors and added a fragrant tree.

Maybe that gypsy had been right. This was where she needed to be, because now she knew that she'd found the road back to living, not just going through the motions.

Turning, she saw Trent gazing at her. She hadn't forgotten he was there, but while she was ready to bring her rooms in Redmond back to life, he was part of the reason she was ready to begin living again.

~*~

Trent drove carefully through the town, taking Whitney back to her cottage. She sat quietly, a small smile on her lips as he negotiated the roads.

What was it about her that spoke to him more than any other woman? He didn't know. He only knew that he wanted her to stay. He wanted her fear of the amusement park to subside. It bothered him that Whitney disliked the one place he thought of as the best on earth.

Trent parked at the curb and jumped down from the cab to help Whitney out. She smiled as she accepted his hands and he set her on her feet. As they walked along the path to her door, he had an idea.

"Whitney, I have something I want you to do."

"Yes?" she said, holding onto the word.

Trent stopped and faced her. "I want you to go for a ride with me."

"Sure," she agreed. "Where to?"

Trent didn't answer immediately. He waited for Whitney to understand this was a serious request. She looked up at him.

"I want you to ride the Ferris wheel."

Holding her hand, he felt her freeze at his words.

"It's the only way. If you want to conquer your fear and reclaim your power, you're going to have to get on it." She was about to refuse, but Trent stopped her. "I'll be with you. I'll hold your hand or let you hide your face in my shoulder." He put his hand on his coat to demonstrate. "It'll be a first step."

"First?"

He could hear the fear in her voice. "I don't expect you to get over your fear with one ride." He waited for her to process the request. "Try it, Whitney."

"I'm afraid," she admitted.

Trent nearly smiled. He thought of the cliché that said admitting that a problem existed was the first step in solving it.

"Just say you're going to try it. We can go to the park and if you absolutely refuse to get on the ride, I won't force you."

"Promise?"

"Cross my heart."

Chapter 6

Why didn't it snow today? Whitney thought. Why couldn't a blizzard come through Christmas Town and shut everything down, including or especially the amusement park? What was wrong with her? Why had she agreed to go to the park and ride that Ferris wheel? Trent held her hand, and while the temperature was in the forties and her hands were inside fleece-lined gloves, her fingers were as cold as ice.

This was her third trip to the park with Trent. She could see the huge goliath rising into the white-blue sky.

"Are you ready?" he asked.

No, her mind screamed, but she nodded.

"You don't have to if it's too scary." Trent gave her a way out.

Whitney wouldn't take it. She'd taken the easy way for the last year. She was no longer going to do that. Life offered challenges, and running from them now would mean she'd run forever.

"I'm not afraid," she said, using a voice stronger than her insides recognized.

Trent got in the car first. The attendant helped Whitney as she took her place. He pulled the safety bar down and locked it. Whitney took a long breath. She was trapped, locked into the seat. There was no going back now.

"It's going to be all right," Trent whispered to her.

She nodded, but didn't totally believe him. She wanted this to be over.

She grabbed Trent's leg as the car swung backwards and stopped to let the next group of holiday-makers on. They were a happy group of three girls. Trent pried Whitney's hand from the safety bar. He said nothing.

"I'm sorry," Whitney apologized.

He pulled her closer and she huddled against him. Looking out on the crowd, she watched as one after another, groups of happy riders, took their places. The car swung back and forth. The higher up it went, the more suspended she felt. Whitney looked through the line at the rosy-cheeked faces. Then she saw something. Sitting straight up, she moved her head, weaving it back and forth trying to see through the people at someone she thought she recognized.

"What is it?" Trent asked, leaning forward.

After a moment, Whitney knew she was wrong. She thought she'd seen the gypsy fortune teller, but the woman who moved through the crowd looked nothing like her when she turned around.

"Nothing," Whitney said. "I thought I saw someone, but I was wrong."

"Who did you see?"

"It doesn't matter. It wasn't anyone I knew."

The car jerked and she clutched the bar. They were too high for her to get off. It took another five agonizing minutes for the rest of the cars to be loaded with riders. Then the music began and the cars started to circle. Wind whipped her hair. Her stomach was as tight as a coil and she was afraid. The urge to close her eyes and turn her face into Trent's shoulder was strong. She forced herself to keep them open, to look at what was happening, to see everything.

They completed the first circle, going all the way to the top and coming down. Whitney let out a breath after the first revolution. She didn't know how many more she had to endure before the ride came to a stop and they could get off. They passed the exit and started up again. Whitney tried to relax, but her teeth were clenched so tightly she thought they might break. Forcing herself, she opened her mouth. The wind rushed in and choked her. She crouched and Trent pulled her closer.

"This is the last one," he whispered when they started the fifth revolution.

Whitney relaxed a bit. She was ready to get off. She wanted the ride to stop.

No sooner had she had the thought, but the wheel jerked several times and complied with her request. They stopped at the top. Panic rose in her. She twisted her hands together. Sitting up, she looked around.

"What's happening?" Whitney asked, her gaze flipping from

side to side.

Trent looked over the safety railing and down at the ground. Whitney refused.

"I don't know." He spoke softly, concern and confusion in his voice.

"Are people getting off?"

"The bottom car just emptied."

"What was that jerk? Was that normal?" Whitney hadn't ever felt that before on a Ferris wheel. She had the feeling something was wrong. Then she heard the sirens. Taking the chance, she looked down. Fire engines were coming and the wheel hadn't moved to let the next group off.

Grabbing the side of the car and Trent's arm, she pushed back. "We're stuck," she said.

"It's all right," Trent said. "It's probably nothing. We'll be down in a few minutes."

Whitney wondered if he believed that. Her hand was on his arm and she felt the tension there. More people gathered below them. She could hear cries of *what's going on* coming from the passengers in other cars. Someone was banging on the outside of a car ahead of them. A couple of teenagers were forcibly swinging theirs back and forth.

Whitney's stomach clenched.

"Whitney, I'm going to have to leave you," Trent said.

Panic seized her, but she clamped down on it. "You can't. It's too dangerous. You could fall, be killed." Her voice cracked on the last word.

"I have to get all the people down. It's my responsibility."

She knew he was right. Logic told her and she understood being responsible for the lives of others, but she was scared too.

"The fire department is here." She looked down. The ground heaved like a ship pitching in rough waters. Closing her eyes, she took long, calming breaths. Still she could see the ground and the red, swirling lights of the trucks. "You have other engineers. Can't they fix this?"

"Maybe, maybe not. But I don't see them. The ladder on the

fire truck won't reach this high. People are already beginning to panic. I have to go."

Whitney closed her eyes and nodded fast. She was one of the ones panicking.

"Stay here," he said. "Keep the bar in place." He tapped on it. "I'll get you down."

She nodded. "I'll be fine." She knew she needed to assure him of her ability to keep it together so he could think about getting the wheel to work and everyone to safety.

He kissed her hard and fast, then slid up the back of the swinging seat. His body pressed against the safety bar. Whitney braced herself against the swinging seat. Trent got out, slipping his long legs over the metal supports and grabbing them.

Whitney gasped at each of his movements; sure the next one would have him plunging to his death.

As much as Whitney didn't want to look, she couldn't help herself. Leaning forward, she watched Trent scale the support beams. Each step jarred her heart.

There was a small coating of ice on one of the beams. Trent didn't see it until it was too late. He stepped on it and his foot slipped. Whitney reached for him as he tumbled through several metal bars, his hands grabbing for something to hold. Whitney's voice was caught in her throat. She couldn't scream. In her mind she saw Mike falling.

Trent's hand caught a bar and he swung. The crowd took a collective breath. Several people screamed. Whitney wasn't one of them. Trent couldn't hold on. He fell again. This time his legs straddled a bar and he grabbed for purchase. The inertia of his body forced him forward and back, where he hit his head. Whitney watched as he slumped forward. The crowd braced for the unconscious man to slide sideways and fall.

Whitney's scream was lost among those coming from the crowd below. Trent lay precariously on a support beam. He was slipping sideways. Without help he was bound to fall. Pushing any thought of danger aside, Whitney was out of her seat and over the bar. The moment she looked down, visions of Mike lying on the ground accosted her. Squeezing both her hands and her eyes, she took a moment to calm herself.

"This isn't Mike," she said out loud. Mike was gone. She couldn't help him. But she could save Trent. She wouldn't let this happen again.

Time was not on her side, but Whitney didn't want to fall prey to the same fate as Trent. Taking care to secure her hold and watch her footing, she moved quickly down the metal structure. The wind was cold and whipped her hair. Glancing down, she saw Trent move again. He was teetering, his body moving with the wind and the vibration of the Ferris wheel.

The fire engine couldn't reach the side he was on. Men below shed their equipment, but were hampered by heavy boots and coats. *She* had to reach him.

Moving faster, and clamping her teeth together, she told herself she was going to make it. Just two more beams, she chanted in her head. She wasn't going to make it. He was listing like a sinking ship. Whitney knew she had to get to him in the next few seconds or he'd fall over the side. Taking her heart in her hands, she leaped across the last beam and caught the bar as she'd done countless times before on the uneven bars.

Sliding down she straddled the beam. She caught Trent just as his body overbalanced. Whitney held on to him tightly. His weight was greater than hers and she had to keep a strong hold or he'd take her with him and tumble to the ground. She hugged him, breathing hard and thanking God she'd got to him in time. His arms hung limply, but she didn't care. He was alive and they were going to be okay.

Taking a moment to catch her breath, she looked at the crowd. Vertigo accosted her as the ground started to yo-yo. Dizziness blurred her eyes. She would not fall. She would not let Trent fall. Closing everything else out, Whitney held onto Trent.
Concentrating on nothing but saving the two of them, she pushed him away slightly and tapped his face to wake him. He opened his eyes, but he was groggy. He couldn't focus. He closed them, dropping his head on her shoulder as he passed out again.

"The ladder is coming," someone called to her.

The fire engine below rolled closer to the Ferris wheel. A white bucket extended from the top of the ladder.

"Steady," someone said from behind her. "We'll take him."

She stopped moving. Suddenly, she felt the wind. It was cold and she was freezing. Her hands felt glued to the metal bar she clung to. Trent was taken from her, just like Mike. She sagged against the support beam.

"We have him. Your turn."

She let the fireman take her, and then she was in the bucket with Trent and two firemen. The ladder began to descend. Whitney didn't see it. She was sitting on the floor, her arms wrapped around the man she'd fallen in love with.

Trent heard a groan and realized it was coming from him. Everything ached, his head, his arms. Even his eyes felt gritty. What had happened to him? He tried to open his eyes, but they were so heavy he wanted to return to sleep.

There was a noise close by. A soft breeze touched his face. He tried to remember what he was doing. Suddenly, it came to him and he tried to sit up. The pain was too intense. It vaulted up the back of his head. Trent flopped back on the pillow. The Ferris wheel. He tried to speak, but couldn't. "What happened...?"

"You fell."

He hadn't known anyone was there. Turning, he tried to see who it was. His eyes opened, but all he saw was a vague shape. Then more shapes arrived, coming in on silent but quick feet.

Someone asked him his name.

"Trent," he said, his voice heavy.

"Last name?"

"Knowles. Who are you?"

Trent opened his eyes again. For a moment the room spun, then settled. Looking around, he recognized a hospital. The sound of monitoring machines verified his thought. He was in a hospital.

He remembered the Ferris wheel. How had he gotten down? How had he gotten here? And where was Whitney? He looked for her, but she was not among the group of people prodding him, looking in his eyes, asking questions, pulling on his fingers and feet.

Trent didn't know when they left, only that he must have fallen asleep again. When he opened his eyes it was dark, and he was alone. At least he thought he was. His head still hurt, but not as much as before. A small light above him created huge shadows in all the corners.

Someone leaned forward, toward his bed. "Whitney?"

"Are you all right?" she asked.

"I'm sorry. I didn't get you down."

She smiled, brushing a tear from her face. Getting up, she came to the bed and took his hand. Trent had seen a lot of angels in Christmas Town, but this was the first time he thought he was looking at a real one.

"How do you feel?" she asked.

"Like an elephant sat on my head."

"You hit it on a metal brace." He raised his free hands and touched a bandage on the back of his head.

"They cut your hair back there. You've got five stitches."

"It feels like they sewed my head to my neck," Trent said.

She laughed; a small tickling sound that didn't carry far, but was the kind you'd hear in hospitals and libraries.

"Did the other people get down safe?"

She nodded. "Everyone is safe. You're the only one who needed medical attention. The engineers found the problem: a new support strut recently installed was put in upside down. It caused the entire mechanism to stall."

Trent pressed his hand into hers. It was soft and he liked the feel of it. He wanted to hold onto her for as long as he could.

She squeezed back.

Chapter 7

The huge Ferris wheel loomed toward the sky. People moved around Whitney without the slightest amount of knowledge that she was contemplating a life-changing event. She watched the lighted amusement ride go through its circular motion. She was afraid, but tonight she was going to go solo. Somehow she'd conquer her beast. If this was the horse that had thrown her, she'd get right back in the saddle. One of them would emerge the winner and she was determined that she would be the one crossing the finish line.

Counting from the front of the line waiting to take a seat on the monstrous Ferris wheel, she was number fifteen. And she was alone. Trent wasn't there to reassure her that she wouldn't relive or repeat two accidents. He'd been released from the hospital, but was confined to bed rest at his house. The line moved, and four teenage girls scampered into the car, all smiles and giggles.

Her stomach felt like it was full of rocks. Her mind told her to run. Her feet were ready, but she took in a long breath and stepped forward.

"One," she said, her voice too low to be heard. The park cast member must have read her lips. He opened the metal bar and took her arm, levering her into the open air seat and locking the bar in place. Whitney slumped against the side of the car. Her hand on her heart, she took long breaths, exhaling through her mouth. The car began to swing upward and she grabbed the safety bar.

She was the last person to get in a car. The wheel's revolutions began. Whitney forced herself to keep her eyes open. The car rode backwards, then up. She looked over the park, then down onto the ground. Neither Mike nor Trent lay there. Her breath slowed from pants to hiccups, then to heavy heaves. Finally, it began to normalize.

Lifting her face up, she let the cold wind brush her skin. Her stomach dropped as the wheel made a downward whoosh. It wasn't a fearful sound. It was normal. The way a person should feel. The way she had felt before Mike died. The wind forced water from her eyes, but it wasn't tears. She smiled at the world. The lights below were happy, and she was too. Since Mike's death, Whitney thought she'd never be happy again, but she was.

The ride came to an end. As Whitney accepted a man's hand and exited the small craft, she felt that the woman who'd gotten into the car wasn't the same as the one who stepped out of it. She was hungry for life. Looking around, she wanted to go on another ride. Challenge the laws of physics and hang upside down two stories above the ground.

Not giving herself time to think about it, she turned quickly, too quickly. She ran directly into Trent.

"Trent, what are you doing here?"

"I own this park," he said with a facetious smile. He wore sunglasses, but still squinted and he listed slightly to the left.

Whitney rushed to steady him. "You haven't been out of the hospital for more than a day and you have a concussion."

"I won't stay long," he said. "But the more important question is why are *you* here? And what were you doing up there?"

They both turned and looked at the giant Ferris wheel. Its lights winked at her. She felt as if they were smiling.

"I needed to prove I could do it."

"You'd already done it," he said.

"With you holding my hand, or more likely, with me gripping yours in a vice."

Trent raised his hands and flexed them, testing to make sure they were still useable.

"I was about to go on another ride, but I think it would be better if I made sure you got home safely. We don't want another accident."

"I'm all right."

She frowned. "Don't tell me you're going to be the typical male?"

"Typical?" His brows rose.

She took his arm and turned him toward the exit. "Typical

guys are invulnerable. You've just gotten out of the hospital. I'm sure the doctor did not release you to return to work." She waited a second to see if he denied it. He said nothing. "So if you do what you're supposed to, you'll be back on your feet soon."

"And if I don't?"

"You'll have me to contend with." She shook his arm and laughed.

The two began to walk back toward the entrance. Whitney watched as people walked around them. But not only around them. There was a spot of ground, a square that no one walked through. There was nothing there, but people moved around it as if there were.

"What's with this spot?" she asked Trent.

He looked at the place where she pointed.

"This is the place where I saw the fortune teller. There was a booth here. The one I told you no one saw except me."

Whitney went to the place he mentioned and stood in front of it. She put her hand up, cautiously extending it in the invisible air. It passed through the segment where the booth had stood. There was nothing to stop it. There didn't appear to be anything in the small square of bricked-over earth. Yet the park patrons walked around the area and neither Whitney nor Trent understood the reason.

~*~

Happy to be inside her warm, temporary home, she began packing. As she placed each sweater, pair of pants, socks and shoes into the suitcase, she told herself she was doing the right thing. Her life was in Redmond. His was here. He had a large, loving family. She had friends, but no loved ones. She had a business to run and so did he. All of that was logical and made sense, but the most glaring reason was that Ferris wheel she couldn't get out of her mind and the image of Trent teetering on the support structure.

Riding it a second time hadn't erased her memory of the accidents. In another second, he would have fallen. And a moment after that he'd be dead or critically ill. Could she put herself through that again?

"Nooo," she said aloud and sat down on the bed next to the suitcase she was packing.

She needed safety. She needed to know that was how things would turn out. That at the end of the day, there would be no mishaps, no danger.

Life doesn't work that way. She heard the therapist's words in her head. All the clichés about the accident came to her. She, or someone she loved, could get hurt doing everyday things. Life had no safety net, and to shut herself off from the possibility of an accident was an impossible mission. Feelings had no switch. She couldn't avoid a connection to another human being. Trent had entered her life, and feelings for him had surfaced and taken root. As much as she denied it or wanted to deny them, there was no putting them aside.

Whitney knew that when she came to Christmas Town, the baggage of Mike's death had arrived with her. In the last few days, she'd emptied the suitcases of her guilt over Mike's fall. But she'd refilled them just as tight and full with feelings and images of Trent.

~*~

Mother Nature wasn't playing fair. At least Whitney didn't think so. When she opened her eyes the next morning, the world outside was not only white, it was impossible to see through. The snowfall had turned to a raging blizzard. Snow outside had piled up higher than her car, and her door might as well be soldered closed.

She was picking up her cell phone when it rang in her hand. Trent's name appeared on the screen. Her heart lurched.

"Trent?"

"Are you all right?" he asked.

"Me? I'm fine. What about you?"

"I meant the snow. Are you all right?"

"I'm snowed in, I think." she said. "The front door is a wall of snow and from the side I can see cars that are completely covered, mine included."

"What about heat and water?"

"The heat is on. I haven't tried the water." As she spoke, she walked to the bathroom and turned on the water in the sink. It poured fully and freely. "The water appears to be fine."

"Good." She heard him sigh as if in relief.

"What about you? Is everything all right there?"

"We're fine."

"And how do you feel?"

"My mother is hovering as if I'm a broken bird, so I'm in good hands." His laugh relaxed her. There were times Whitney wished she had a mother to hover over her. While other women complained about their mothers, Whitney would relish the idea of having a mother always around, even if they disagreed. There would always be love between them, and it would remain unconditional.

"I suppose you're all enjoying being together."

"We are," he laughed. "It can get a little claustrophobic at times, but we love each other." Trent's family had arrived as soon as they heard about his accident.

"I know. I could see it in the way you all look at and help each other."

"Your life has been different," he stated.

Whitney didn't say anything.

"It won't always be that way," Trent added.

He couldn't know that, but she didn't think this was the time to get into it. "I thought I'd get on the road today. There won't be much traffic. I can make it back to Redmond later tonight if I leave now."

"You can't drive in this snow. The roads won't be clear for a day or two."

She heard something in his voice. Concern was the underlining, but it wasn't the main thread. Could it be panic?

"Once I can get out of the cabin, the roads will probably be clear. I'll check the weather station before leaving."

"I thought you came here to spend the holiday."

"That wasn't my original plan. I told you why I came here, but I think my purpose has been fulfilled. It's time to go home."

"What purpose?" he asked.

Whitney didn't have a real answer for that question. "I have the feeling that I'm supposed to be in Redmond. That there's something there I need to take care of. Here, everything seems in order. Staying has no purpose."

"No purpose. Would you stay if I asked you to?"

Was he asking, she wondered? Again, her heart began to thunder, but Whitney quickly tamped it down.

"Trent, I've only been here a little more than a week."

"For some people that could be a lifetime. If you hadn't been here, it would be my lifetime."

"That's not true. The men climbing from the ground would have gotten to you."

"They wouldn't. I watched the video of that accident today. Without you, I'd be on the ground like Mike."

Whitney gasped. She hadn't expected Trent to bring up Mike.

"Whitney, I'm not Mike, and what happened to him didn't happen to me. *You. . .*" He emphasized the word. "You are the reason I'm talking to you on the phone."

She heard the unsaid remainder of his sentence; *if they weren't on the phone, they'd be attending his funeral.* The image she conjured up made her wince.

"Can we talk about something else?"

"You haven't answered my question."

"You didn't ask a question."

"All right, I'll ask. Will you stay for the holiday?"

Everything about his question told her to refuse, but her heart sang a different tune.

"Trent, you have a houseful of guests. You don't need me around to entertain while you have family and friends who need your attention."

"You are the only one whose attention I need."

Whitney had no response. She was out of excuses, and to tell the truth, she really didn't want to leave. She wanted to spend every minute with Trent.

"Well, I can promise I'll be here until the snow clears," she said.

"I'll take that," he replied. "And if I get my way, I'll make sure we have snow until the New Year."

Secretly, Whitney wouldn't mind if she stayed here without snow as long as she could be with him.

Chapter 8

The gates to Knowles Wonderland were closed. Trent stood outside them. His life had changed so much in the last few days. Whitney had come into his world, and nothing would ever be the same.

His gaze went to the Ferris wheel, sitting silent and unmoving in the cold air. It had taken a lot of courage for Whitney to ride it, first with him, then after his accident that nearly mirrored the one in her past, to attack the monster alone.

"You're in love with her."

Trent looked at the woman standing next to him. He hadn't seen or heard her coming, and he didn't know her. Yet there was something familiar about her. And her comment was a statement, not question.

"Hello," he said, wondering if she was a tourist or a relative here for the holiday. It was impossible to determine her age. She had long blonde hair that hung from beneath a red hat. Her face was free of lines and her blue eyes sparkled like someone with a secret they were bursting to share. A long coat the same color as her hat fell to the top of her black boots. She was attractive, but Trent's heart was held by another.

"I see you're out for a stroll this Christmas morning," she said.

"I am."

"And you've spent many wonderful Christmases here."

Again it was a statement. Trent frowned. "Excuse me, but have we met before? I'm Trenton Knowles."

"We've met many times," she said, but did not give a name.

"Where? I apologize, but I don't remember. Are you visiting someone here?"

She nodded. "Two people actually."

It was on the tip of his tongue to ask who, but he held back. Christmas Town was small, but not so small that it was possible to know everyone.

"Well, I have to get back. My family is waiting. I hope you'll enjoy your holiday."

"I'll be leaving soon. My job is finished."

Trent smiled, feeling uncomfortable, but having no reason for it. "Good morning." He turned to leave, but was stopped by the woman's next words.

"She's planning to leave. You could stop that."

"What?"

"All you need to do is ask her."

"Ask who?"

"The woman who's on your mind."

Trent immediately thought of Whitney. Not only did she come to mind, but her comments on the strangeness of Christmas Town surfaced. This woman was strange to him. He was sure he'd never met her before, and she was speaking in riddles.

"What do you know about a woman and me?"

She smiled. Her teeth were white and the smile reached her eyes.

"I'll leave you to figure that out, but..." she paused, raising her finger and pointing it at him as any teacher delivering an important point would do,"...I wouldn't wait another minute."

With that she smiled, turned and began a fast walk away. Trent contemplated her words, cryptic as they had been. He looked toward the place where Whitney was staying. It was too far to see, but he thought of her. He wondered how the woman knew Whitney.

He spun around to call her and ask. She was gone. He looked left and right. She wasn't there. The path leading to the park was a sprawling walkway. It stretched back for over fifty yards to the parking lot. It was impossible for her not to be seen.

Yet nothing and no one was in the area. From where he stood to the distant lot, all he saw was twinkling lights and empty air.

Trent started walking. He needed to find Whitney. Suddenly he felt an urgency to find her. He loved her, not because she was brave, but because he needed her. She completed him. She did all the things the clichés said. He wanted her to stay. He wanted her to be there every day when he woke and each evening when he came home. He wanted to understand everything about her, share her life and share his with her.

He had to find her—now!

~*~

Merry Christmas was Whitney's first thought when she woke on Christmas Day. Last night came back to her. She smiled as warmth spread through her system. The cottage was festively decorated, and Christmas Eve with Trent and his family had been a delightful time. Whitney pushed the covers back and sat up. While it was Christmas, it was also her last day in Christmas Town. She had to go back to Redmond.

Back to her life.

Back to her world.

The real one, where she had a business to run, and the livelihood of her employees and their families rested on her. She liked Christmas Town. She wanted to stay, but that was out of the question. Her suitcase was packed. All she needed to do was add her cosmetics. It lay open on the luggage stand as a reminder that she had other obligations. Pushing the thought aside, Whitney decided to dwell on the day and not on what she had to do tomorrow.

She dressed quickly, wearing her new striped socks under a pair of pants. Donning a coat, she headed out for a short walk. She'd taken to doing it every day. With the food she ate, she needed to change that walk to a run.

"Good morning." A woman spoke as Whitney reached the end of the driveway.

"Merry Christmas," Whitney said.

"He's at the entrance to the park," she said and winked before walking away.

Whitney looked at her with a frown, then glanced toward the amusement park. "Who's at the park?" she asked, but the woman was gone. Whitney stood on the sidewalk alone. Nothing moved except the mechanical Christmas decorations.

Taking her car, she headed west, toward the park. Was Trent there? Had the woman meant him?

It didn't take Whitney long to reach the gates. As expected, Trent stood in front of them, clad in the white parka he'd worn the night she met him.

Getting out of the car, she put the keys in her pocket. Her hand touched a scrap of paper and she pulled it out. Trent turned and looked at her. She thought she saw a frown on his face. It quickly turned to surprise.

Pushing the paper back inside her pocket, she approached him.

"How did you know I was here?" he asked.

"The woman told me."

"Woman?"

"Yes, it was strange. I came out for a walk and as I got to the sidewalk she was there, almost of if she'd been waiting for me."

"And she said I was here?" he asked.

Whitney took a second to think about it. "She didn't exactly say *you*. I mean she didn't call you by name. She said...'he's at the park entrance,'" Whitney quoted.

"What did she look like?"

Whitney described her. "I only saw her for a long moment. Then she was gone." Whitney didn't want to say she disappeared into thin air. Trent was frowning. "What's wrong?"

"She was just here. Not two minutes ago. She couldn't have gotten over there in so short a time."

Whitney said nothing.

Whitney thought about the woman, pulling her description to mind. She looked like Mrs. Hamilton, the Mrs. Claus housekeeper that Trent didn't have. Then her features transformed and Whitney clearly saw who she was.

"The fortune teller," she said aloud.

"What about her?" Trent asked.

She looked Trent straight in the eye. "I saw her."

"Where?"

"Here." She indicated the park. "In your house. On the street.

She's the woman in the red coat, your housekeeper and the gypsy. They're all the same woman."

"They can't be." He looked incredulously at her as if she'd lost her mind. Quite the contrary, her mind was clear.

"Think about her," Whitney said, excitement dancing in her blood. "She knew things about us. She brought me here. And here I ran into you. And here, I came back and began to live again. You said you didn't know Mrs. Hamilton, but I saw her. I talked to her. And you've talked to her, yet you can't explain her presence.

She pulled the paper out and handed it to him.

"What's this?"

"Another note. I found it in my pocket."

Trent looked at the words on Christmas notepaper. It read, *The second thing you have to do is find Trenton Knowles.* He looked up at her. "She sent you here to find me?"

"More than that, she sent me here to find my future."

"Did you find it?" he asked.

She heard the apprehension in his voice. Whitney smiled. "I think so. What did she tell you?"

He thought about it so long, Whitney didn't think he remembered. His eyes looked far away. She was unsure if he saw the past or the future.

"What did she tell you?" Whitney asked again.

"Nothing I didn't already know."

"What do you know?"

"I know you're planning to leave tomorrow. I know you have obligations. And I know without the slightest doubt that I'm in love with you."

Whitney was stunned. She couldn't find her voice for the sudden pounding of her heart. She stared at Trent, unable to move, unable to look away, and unable to speak.

"Don't you feel anything for me?" he asked.

She nodded. She tried her voice but it didn't come. Trying again, she said. "I love you, too."

"I want you to stay in Christmas Town. I want you to marry me and spend your life with me."

Whitney might not be able to speak for the emotions that cut off her voice, but she could move. In two steps she wrapped her arms around him and pulled his mouth to hers. She kissed him desperately, like a woman in love. Like a woman who'd found the man of her dreams. They stood like that a long time, happy in knowing they'd merged from being a single entity to being a couple bonded so close together that nothing could separate them.

When Trent broke the kiss, she looked into eyes that were unguarded. Love shone there as clearly and brightly as a second sun.

"Can you still insist there is nothing strange going on here?"

"No," he shook his head. "There is definitely something going on." He paused. "But it's not Christmas Town."

Whitney looked directly at him, waiting for his response.

"It's you...and me and the spirit of Christmas."

"Will it always be that way?" she asked.

"Without a doubt," he said and kissed her.

The End

www.ingramcontent.com/pod-product-compliance
Lightning Source LLC
Chambersburg PA
CBHW020643130626
46552CB00003B/1369